DESCENDANT OF HELL

RICK WOOD

BLOOD SPLATTER PRESS

ABOUT THE AUTHOR

Rick Wood is a British writer born in Cheltenham.

His love for writing came at an early age, as did his battle with mental health. After defeating his demons, he grew up and became a stand-up comedian, then a drama and English teacher, before giving it all up to become a full-time author.

He now lives in Cheltenham, where he divides his time between watching horror, reading horror, and writing horror.

ALSO BY RICK WOOD

The Sensitives
The Sensitives
My Exorcism Killed Me
Close to Death
Demon's Daughter
Questions for the Devil
Repent
The Resurgence
Until the End

Blood Splatter Books
Psycho B*tches
Shutter House
This Book is Full of Bodies
Home Invasion

Rick also publishes thrillers under the pseudonym Ed Grace...

Jay Sullivan

Assassin Down

Kill Them Quickly

The Bars That Hold Me

A Deadly Weapon

Rick Wood
Publishing

For Mum and Dad.

Thank you for your support and love, which I would not have been able to come this far without.

FEBRUARY, 1998

TWO YEARS BEFORE MILLENNIUM NIGHT

CHAPTER ONE

*E*ddie flinched as he burnt his tongue on his coffee to go.

Stupid, damn coffee.

It was too dark to be morning.

The air from the open car window struck his face with a chill that prompted him to wake up. He closed it.

Derek turned the car down a gravel path between two empty fields of dead grass. What a waste. Why not plant some seeds? Grow some crops? Maybe make a vineyard to help stock his shelves with wine? Instead this family had left the fields blank, dank, and depressing.

Derek pulled up at the farmhouse and switched off the engine. He remained still and in thought. Eddie looked at him uncertainly, wondering why they weren't getting out of the car.

"Relax, Eddie. This isn't going to work out if you're too uptight."

Uptight? I couldn't be less uptight. I'm practically asleep, I'm so ungiddy.

It was true, Eddie was lethargic. Not because he wasn't excited to witness his first haunting, he absolutely was — it was

1

because that excitement had kept him up all night and he was running on a mere three hours of sleep.

"Take a moment," Derek instructed, his voice low and calm. "Think about it. Take it in. The presence does not start with the person it's haunting, it ends with them. The real work starts as you approach the house."

Eddie rubbed his eyes and attempted to make sense of what Derek had just said. He knew it was true, he knew it was helpful; God, he even knew it was wise. But it was too early to be forcing his mind to comprehend so many words.

"Wh-what?" he prompted as a response.

"You have a gift, Eddie. I have to rely on inkling alone, but with you, we know you are able to pick up on these things. So pick up on it. What do you feel?"

What do I feel? Hmm. What do I feel...

"I kinda need the toilet, to be honest. That coffee…"

"Eddie, focus!"

"Fine."

He gave his head a shake, cleared his mind, and closed his eyes. He focussed on his breathing, on remaining calm, on thinking with clarity. Against his best intentions, he found himself drifting back to sleep. His eyes became heavy and his mind began to drift…

THWACK! That's when it hit him. His head jolted upright, his eyes shot open, and his whole body paralysed. His surroundings left him at lightning speed and all he could see and feel was the inside of the bedroom, up the stairs of the house and to the second door on the right.

He saw a girl.

But, it wasn't a girl.

At least, he could tell it was a girl's body, but what was there was…

He retched. Whatever it was made him feel ill; it was unnatural. He could smell burning, but not normal burning — it felt like someone had lit an incense candle that gave off a foul stench and filled him with hatred. Anger surged through his body like cocaine, filling him from the top of his head and to the tip of his toes with a sense of greed and disdain for the world.

He saw inside this girl. He could see her in there, screaming, desperately reaching out, but she was tiny, a minuscule version of herself oppressed by a giant red claw with rotting fingernails.

With a violent jolt, his body shuddered and he spewed up a mouthful of blood, spraying it over the dashboard of the car. Panting heavily, he lent his hand forward as he regained consciousness, his eyes shooting wide open.

"Er... sorry about the..." Eddie began, gesturing to the red liquid he had brought up moments before. Everything spun. His arms were shaking like he was cold, which contradicted the sweat trickling down his forehead.

"It's okay, Eddie, just relax. You've had what we call a vision."

"A vision?"

If that's what they were calling it, he'd rather not. He felt like he'd just been on a rollercoaster ride.

"Yes, they are harmless, really."

"Harmless?" Eddie heard himself replying in a pitch higher than he expected. "Fricking harmless? Have you ever had a vision?"

"No, I'm not able to."

"Right, then — no vision, no opinion."

He pushed the car door open and fell to his knees. He coughed up more blood and used the car to drag himself to his feet. His panting gradually subsided, his shaking ceased, and he regained control over his body.

"What did you see?" asked Derek, who had somehow made his way out of the car and to Eddie's side.

"The girl, in there, it's not her. I mean, it's her, but it's not. Something has her. And she's trapped inside, and she's scared, and she's—"

"Okay, Eddie, that's great, you did great."

With a patronising yet reassuring pat on the back, Derek left Eddie to collect his bag from the boot. He lugged it over his shoulder and carried it to the door, waving Eddie to follow before producing a loud, clear knock on the front door.

Eddie's agreement to be here was down to his admiration for Derek, and Derek's unfaltering belief in what Eddie was capable of. But he had never been warned about getting visions that practically gave him a seizure.

"You think I'm going to have more of them?" Eddie screeched at Derek, still not able to calm his voice. He pushed himself to his feet and stumbled to Derek's side.

"Yes. As you get used to them, they will become easier and you'll gain more control."

Gain more control?

The door opened, revealing a solemn, middle-aged man and woman standing before them. Their hair was unkempt, their clothes bore patchy stains, and grey, faded skin drooped beneath their blood-shot eyeballs.

"Good morning. My name is Derek, and this is Edward. May we come in?"

"Please," replied the man, showing them inside.

The woman obliged Derek's request for a cup of tea, and the man indicated for them to sit in the living room. They perched on the edge of the sofa as the couple introduced themselves as Julie and Dawson.

Julie handed Eddie a cup of tea that looked so weak he dreaded drinking it. It was practically milk and hot water, with a little light-brown tinge to it. He already hated it here.

"So, is it Larissa…?" Derek prompted.

"Yes, she is upstairs, in her room," Julie said. "We daren't go in there anymore."

She turned her head away and sobbed.

"The door normally just slams in our face," Dawson continued, rubbing his wife's back and turning his concerned grimace to Derek. "And if we even manage to get in there, it isn't long before it starts attacking us, or itself."

"Any brothers or sisters?"

"An older brother and an older sister. They are with Julie's parents. When Larissa attacked our boy, she left a large cut across his cheek, so we decided it was best they stayed away."

Derek nodded and took a sip of his tea. Eddie watched to see if Derek reacted with the same repulsion for the awfully made beverage that Eddie had. Derek managed to hide it quite well, but after his initial sip he placed it upon the table with a clear decision not to touch it again.

"May we see Larissa?"

"Of course." The father rose from his seat.

"Alone?"

Dawson froze in mid-rise, glanced at Julie, then turned to Derek and reluctantly nodded. Derek smiled a warm, reassuring smile. He nodded at Eddie and led him upstairs.

As Eddie had seen in his vision, the girl was in the second door to the right at the top of the stairs. The floorboards creaked beneath Eddie's step and he felt loose nails press into the soles of his feet. The brown, tasteless wallpaper peeled off the haggard walls, and the more they approached the room, the colder it became. Eddie could see his breath in the air.

As they entered the bedroom, the entity that dwelled within Larissa's body lifted its head with a sadistic smirk. It cackled at the sight of them.

It croaked a long, drawn-out laugh, in a deep, snarling voice, wriggling and writhing all over the bed.

"Well," it said. "They sent an exorcist."

5

It continued laughing; that is, until Eddie entered the room. Then it fell silent. Completely still. Its eyes glazed over into wide-eyed terror, its jaw sinking and terror overcoming its face.

"It's you…" it marvelled.

Eddie glanced at Derek. He wasn't expecting this. Derek looked unnerved also.

"You have returned…"

"Returned?" Eddie said. "I was never here."

In an abrupt movement, the girl's body flung off the bed and scarpered past Eddie and Derek, thudding down the stairs. They sprinted after her, urgently, practically skidding off the bottom step and accelerating toward the garden, following the girl's shadow.

They found the glass door to the garden smashed, and a red trail of footprints leading across the paving slabs, the damp blood glistening in the moonlight.

They slowed down, cautiously edging onto the patio. A rustling came from across the garden.

The shed.

With one wary foot in front of the other, he inched forward. Once he had reached the shed, he opened the door, and peered in.

The girl shot a nail gun through one of her hands and into the shed wall. A nail flew from the nail gun to her other hand, and she hung there, pinned to the walls.

Eddie knew what this was. Her hands were pinned up like she was on a cross. It was mocking the words he had used against her. It was mimicking stigmata.

"Stop!" Eddie cried out, aware of the pain this must be causing the girl hidden inside.

The grey face lifted, grinning at Eddie.

"You have finally come," it said.

The terror on the face of the demon had turned to glee. It was practically dancing.

"You have come. And now you can command us."

Eddie stared. He glanced at Derek, who also appeared stumped.

He had no idea what the demon was talking about.

"Even Satan disguises himself as an angel of light"
(2 Corinthians 11:14)

JULY, 2001

ONE YEAR, SEVEN MONTHS SINCE MILLENNIUM
NIGHT

CHAPTER TWO

A big sigh fell out of Jason's mouth. Thirty years was a long time to have been doing this, but he had become very, very good at it; now, he was too good to give it up and retire.

He didn't feel quite as observant and energetic as he once had, but he was still keen nonetheless. That passion for making sure people knew the truth, and making sure people were not manipulated, was still there.

"I'm getting a C," claimed 'Psychic Phil,' the wondrous, magnificent con-artist. "I'm getting a C from over here, is there anyone who is linked with a C..."

He waved his hand in a swirling motion over the opposite side of the stalls to where Jason was sitting. It was amazing to him that people still needed to be told that this was a load of crap. Surely they don't think some knobhead shouting "I'm getting a C!" over a crowd of around three-hundred gullible idiots was evidence for some psychic phenomenon. If anything, it was evidence for how much people will believe something when they are desperate to believe it.

A middle-aged man wearily rose his hand, glancing nervously around.

"Ah!" exclaimed Psychic Phil. "Stand up, my friend."

The man rose, his hands fidgeting, timidly looking around at the sea of faces staring back at him.

"But your name is not what the C is about, your name is... what is your name, my friend?"

"Paul."

"Paul!" he repeated with a grand gesture of his arms, flinging them out to convey wonder to his audience. "And I am getting a very strong C, possibly a cat something, car, cur, maybe crocro-"

"Calippo?"

"That is it! Tell me, what is Calippo to you?"

"It was my grandfather's favourite ice cream."

"Ah, I see! And your grandfather is not with us any more, is that true?"

"No, he is not."

Paul looked amazed that this man was able to pick up on such extraordinary facts about his life. Calippo was his dead grandparents favourite ice cream? *Hold the phone!* thought Jason.

He sat back and rubbed his hand over his forehead. This guy wasn't even making an effort. Over his years, Jason had found psychics with ear-pieces, psychics who had done thorough research on their audiences, psychics who had risen into the air and added some theatricality to their stupidity. Not this guy. This guy was just reliant on good, old-fashioned cold-reading — and really, really bad cold-reading at that.

"And your grandfather, yes, he's coming through to me now Paul, he's coming through..." Psychic Phil put his fingers on his temples and bowed his head, closing his eyes, showing immense concentration. "Yes, Paul, he's telling me — 'don't worry about the mess.' Does that mean anything to you?"

"Yes!" Paul gasped, putting his hand on his chest to show his shock. "Yes, my grandfather left the family in quite a mess."

"Excellent, Paul, excellent, you're doing great; but wait! I have something else coming through! He says, 'it's time to let me go, Paul.' Do you know what that might mean?"

Jason scoffed, more loudly than he'd intended. *It's time to let me go... don't worry about the mess...* Was this man in so much grief that he'd actually believe this bullshit? As if someone from the beyond would ever say it *wasn't* time to let them go.

Jason went a little red. He felt embarrassed for Paul. He was obviously craving closure with his dead relative; so much that he was forcing himself to believe all that was being said.

Enough was enough. It was time for Jason to show this fraud for what he was.

"Right, I'm getting an M from over here," Psychic Phil started circling his hand over the area of the audience Jason was sat in. Without hesitating, Jason lifted his hand in the air.

"Thank you, my child, please stand."

Jason obliged, smiling sarcastically, and placing his hands in his pockets.

"I'm getting a Ma, maybe a Margaret, or a Marissa?"

"Miranda," Jason stated bluntly.

"What?"

"My dead wife. Her name was Miranda."

Psychic Phil performed a moment of concentration, scrunching his face, before continuing with his act.

"Right, yes, Miranda – and she died of some sort of illness, am I right?"

"Yes, cancer."

Some of the audience around him gasped, looking at him sympathetically.

"Yes, she's coming through to me now, she has something to say…"

"And what is that?"

15

"I'm getting red, the colour red... does that mean anything?"

"Her blood was red."

"Her blood was red? Right, well it may be something else, we'll see... Yes, and now she's saying... Yes, she's saying... 'Please don't cry for me.' Do you know what that might mean?"

"Yes. When she died, I cried."

"Oh my!" Psychic Phil stood back, aghast. "Thank you, you may sit."

"Just before I do, Mr Phil, Psychic, whatever-" Jason raised his hand to halt Psychic Phil, who froze, his eyes shifting nervously. This wasn't in the script. "I have something to say about my dear wife."

"Oh yes?"

"She isn't real. I made her up."

The theatre fell into complete and utter silence. People looked back and forth from Jason to Psychic Phil, like an intense tennis match. The tension grew hostile.

"Why, whatever do you mean?" Psychic Phil turned wide-eyed, attempting to save his show.

"You just gave me a reading for a dead woman who never lived or died. You just told me what she said, and she never existed."

Psychic Phil looked over his shoulder, evidently at someone backstage, with an expression that said 'what do I do?'

"So you lied?" Psychic Phil shook his head, disappointed. "Oh, how dare you."

"How dare *I* lie?" Jason raised his voice in anger but smiled, enjoying the moment. "You have just lied to every person in here. You have just told me you heard my dead wife talking to me through you, and that was a lie. You told me you were picking up on her, and that was a lie. And you dare to call *me* the liar?"

Psychic Phil backed away toward the wings. Boos rang out through the theatre, heckles and jeers directed at the stage.

"You have committed fraud today, and these people deserve their money back."

The crowd echoed Jason's words, repeatedly chanting: "We want our money back!" Oh, how tables can turn; one minute they were lapping it up, then a simple explanation from a man who had been doing this for years turned them all against Psychic Phil.

Jason made his way through the row of seats between him and the aisle, bearing a grin, enjoying the sound of an audience defiant to the psychic, who had since scampered off-stage and dumped his microphone.

Pleased with his day's work, he put his coat on and left the theatre. The sun was still shining in the cool summer sky and he enjoyed a nice, quiet walk home.

SEPTEMBER, 2001

ONE YEAR, NINE MONTHS SINCE MILLENNIUM
NIGHT

CHAPTER THREE

*K*elly's train pulled up late morning and she loaded herself up like a pack mule. She held a suitcase to her right that she could wheel along, a suitcase in her other hand she could carry, a stuffed sports bag over her back, and her carry-on bag on her shoulder. No one gave any sympathy to her struggles off the train; they simply barged past her, knocking her off balance again and again.

No, Dad, I don't need a lift... I'd rather do it myself... I've taken the train before, I'll be fine...

She felt like a right plonker. Just because she didn't want her parents to embarrass her in front of her new flat mates, she had subjected herself to clumsy shambles along the train station platform, loaded with bags she could drop at any moment. She felt like a human Jenga; if one piece went, so would all the rest.

She made it to the bus outside the station, spotting all the people who had barged past her leering at her out the window of the bus she'd just missed. What a bunch of dicks! That's people for you, just a bunch of selfish voyeurs. See a young lady struggling, do you help? No! You stare gormlessly.

They next bus arrived and she fumbled for her purse in her carry-on bag, using the spare fingers of a hand already clutching her suitcase. With great difficulty, and a few impatient huffs from the waiting bus driver, she withdrew the money, paid him, and dumped herself on a seat. She lay all her items on the seat beside her, leant her head back, closed her eyes, and sighed. That may have only been a short walk loaded up with all her belongings, but it had already knackered her out.

She glanced at herself in the reflection of the window, wiping her face with her hands, catching a whiff of perspiration caused by her bag-carrying ordeal. She did not want to have to meet everyone with her hair and forehead dripping with sweat and big pit stains beneath her armpits. She lifted her arms subtly, trying to sneak a look, and noticed a slightly wet circle underneath each pit.

She threw her head back and closed her eyes again, forcing herself to chuckle at the situation. She had to. The alternative was to cry. And she did not want to turn up with wet eyes as well as wet pits.

She was a genuinely pretty woman; only nineteen, but looked younger than she was. She wasn't someone who needed makeup and hair extensions, which was good, as she despised having to apply such things. She had freckles over her nose and long, auburn hair that glided off her shoulders like wind off a mountain. She had an impressive physique, especially since she had started running that summer. She'd had to; if she had spent another minute growing restless indoors, watching television with her parents, she would have lost it.

She gazed at the town as it floated by the window of the bus. There was a large park where a group of boys were playing Frisbee. She had heard about the university's Ultimate Frisbee society; it had been described on the student union page of their website as 'legendary.' Kelly had always found describing something as legendary a little farfetched. She had loved stories of King Arthur, Knights of the Round Table and Greek gods as a child, so much so her dad had bought her an encyclopaedia of the Greek gods for her ninth birthday. All these people performing heroic acts, such as pulling a sword out of stone, or rescuing a woman they loved; *they* were legendary. Someone throwing a Frisbee back and forth? Not sure that could match slaying a dragon.

The bus paused to pick up a few more people. Among them were a group of people who looked her age, with baggy jeans and shoulder bags, sporting the typical student look. She smiled. After a year out, she had been desperate to finally get started in her psychology degree.

It occurred to her she was going to need an explanation as to what she did on her gap year. What do most people do? Build a school in some war-torn country? Go travelling to find yourself? Get a job?

She didn't know what to go with, but she knew she wouldn't be able to tell the truth. She could imagine how that conversation would go.

"Hi, I'm Kelly. So what did you do on your year out?"

"Ah, well I worked at a café for a few months, then travelled along Europe before settling in the Middle East, where I helped a small village in a war-torn country rebuild their homes. It was amazing. What about you?"

"That's lovely. Yeah, so I was sectioned, spent ten months in a mental health facility, got so numbed on medication that I couldn't function, and finally got released when I had managed to regain a sense of what is real and what is not. I currently take three pills a day as part of a post-sectioning treatment program. These scars on my arm? Yeah, I was sectioned after I tried to kill myself. It was amazing. So, you fancy going for a drink?"

Yes, that was not a conversation she wished to have. She

would need to think of something. She didn't want people to automatically assume she was crazy. Maybe once she got to know people, she could be honest. Until then, it was probably best not to be.

The bus pulled up outside the halls of residence. She reloaded herself with all her bags and hobbled off the bus, into the car park. She had barely hobbled a few steps before a man in a purple t-shirt rushed over to her.

"Hi, how you doing?" He smiled. He was a good-looking guy, with his hair slicked to the side and his teeth perfectly whitened. "Let me give you a hand with that."

He took her shoulder bag and the suitcase from her hand and tucked it under his arm, casually walking alongside her. She noticed that there were a lot of other people wearing purple helping to carry bags. The place was alive with an infectious buzz, rammed with people unloading cars and taking their belongings into their new dorms. Cars were queueing to get into the car park and people dressed in purple were trying to organise their parking.

"I'm Doug." He smiled at Kelly sweetly, making her knees go slightly weak. "I'm in my second year, studying English Literature. What's your name?"

"Kelly," she answered, half-giggling, half-staring, making her name come out in an embarrassing snort.

"Hi, Kelly, which halls are you in?"

"Er… Newton."

"Awesome. This way."

He led her into a courtyard in the middle of a square of buildings. Each section had the name of a famous genius on it. She spotted Darwin and Einstein next to her new halls, Newton.

"Well, I'll leave you here, Kelly," Doug announced, placing her bags outside of the door leading to Newton. "Don't forget to collect your keys first."

She attempted to smile and ended up giggling like a loon. Two minutes there and she was already awkwardly bumbling over a good-looking guy.

She heeded Doug's instructions and collected her keys from the office at the front of the court yard. They had a label reading *13 Newton.*

"Thirteen. Unlucky for some..." she muttered to herself.

She lugged her bags up the stairs to the second floor and found her way to number thirteen. She let herself in and dumped everything on the bed, then propped the door open behind her. It was a small room, but it would do the job. A big welcome box sat on the bed, a desk was propped against the wall, and the metal bars coming off the bed-frame gave her a flashback to her time in the facility.

That bed had made it feel like prison, as did the small space and the confined walls.

"Hey!" came a chirpy voice from behind Kelly. She spun around quickly and smiled.

"Hi."

"I'm Mindy," introduced the person in front of Kelly, a little too eagerly. She had a flower stuck in her brown hair, wore a strappy top with a little too much cleavage, and a long, flowing, flowery skirt. She struck Kelly as hippie-ish, and her overly enthusiastic nature only added to such an image.

"I'm Kelly," she answered, taking Mindy's outstretched hand and shaking it.

"It's so lovely to meet you," Mindy declared, patting her hands on her knees and bending slightly as she did. "I can't wait for us to go out together."

"I'm sure it's going to be great. I could do with a drink now, to be honest."

"Me, too!" Mindy gasped, as if this was the most delightfully shocking news she had ever heard. "Let's go to the student union bar."

Kelly followed Mindy out of her room, leaving behind the bed, an undetected stink of damp, and enclosed walls that reminded her of the familiar feelings of being strapped to a bed so she could not harm herself from things that were never there.

OCTOBER, 1999

TWO MONTHS BEFORE MILLENNIUM NIGHT

CHAPTER FOUR

$\mathcal{E}$ddie and Derek carried themselves in silence to the wooden bench at the edge of the garden. Inside the house, doting parents and three tireless sisters lovingly embraced their younger brother. They cried tears of joy; the stress and disaster of the past few months turned into uncontrollable grief and happiness. They had no idea how to handle those emotions, but it didn't matter. Their adoring son and faithful brother had returned from the ownership of a demon, thanks to the two strangers who had fought for three nights straight to free him.

It was another success for Eddie and Derek, the fifteenth that year. They were getting used to the accolade and triumph of defeating an entity of hell, but they were exhausted — it was taking its toll.

They slumped down and panted, not talking, taking a few minutes to let their heavy breathing subside and for them to collect their thoughts. It was gone four in the morning and the smell of rain was in the air, but they didn't care. The cold breeze was a luxury that cooled their sweaty faces, and the rain washed away their perspiration.

Eddie had never seen Derek so scruffy. Usually, he had his tie done up to the top, his waistcoat smartly affixed, and his shirt tucked in. Right now, his tie was hanging down, his waistcoat laid scruffily over his shoulder, and his shirt half hung out. This entity had been a bastard and they both looked — and felt — like they had taken on hell itself.

And, of course, in a way, they had.

"Fuck. Me." Eddie finally broke the silence. His shaking was finally receding, his breathing returning to normal, and he could once again feel the coolness of the air.

"I don't normally verbalise such brash statements," Derek said. "But in this case, I would concur — fuck me indeed."

Eddie chuckled to himself. That was the first time he had heard the man swear and, honestly, it sounded a little funny coming from his voice.

Inside the garden window they could see the family still embracing in tears, clutching onto their youngest for dear life.

"Think they are ever going to thank us?" Eddie said.

"In time, dear boy, in time. Let them just be happy for a moment. And let us relax, that one was…"

There was no good way to finish that sentence; there were no words Derek could think of to describe an exorcism that had lasted three nights. He had heard of such a thing lasting weeks, but he had so rarely taken more than a night, especially since Eddie had gotten involved. In fact, since Eddie had come on the scene, the exorcisms had barely lasted a few hours. Eddie had a knack for being able to know when it was a real haunting and not someone's deteriorating mental health, which was a huge time saver, and allowed them to intervene far earlier than Derek previously had. What's more, demons seemed to be instantly obedient to Eddie's every instruction, so much so Derek couldn't quite comprehend it.

"I've got a question," Eddie spoke into the gentle night breeze.

"Yes?"

"What is it about me that means I can command demons so well?"

It was a good question, and one that Derek had often wondered about.

"Sometimes people just have such gifts, I guess."

"It can't be that simple, surely. I mean, I know sometimes some people may just have a talent for something, but it's the things these demons say."

"Such as?"

Eddie sighed and tried to think of an example. It happened so consistently that it was hard to think of a specific thing said to him now he was put on the spot.

"Well… 'it's you.' How often is it a demon has said to me, 'it's you'?"

"Maybe they have an in-built inclination, something that helps them recognise when they are faced with a person who has such abilities."

"No, because it isn't, like, 'oh, you have so much power.' They are saying, 'you.' Like I am someone they know. Or some*thing* they know."

Derek started to answer then stopped. Eddie had a point. How was it that the demons always addressed him as if they knew him? How was it they always did what he said so easily?

"Maybe this is something we ought to consider, Eddie. Something we can research and hypothesise at the university. I'm sure Levi will have his two cents."

"Yeah, sure…" Eddie supposed that was the best he could get, really; Derek promising he would consider it and exploring some theories. He just felt like such a question should be more than an experiment or a paper he was writing.

These things seemed to know who he was, to the point they were addressing him on almost personal terms. He was getting more than frustrated with it, but Derek wasn't to blame. If anything, Derek was the one who had encouraged his abilities, put him on the right path, and showed him what he could do. Derek wasn't the one to get annoyed with.

"I just…" He wanted to make Derek understand how he felt, but the words didn't come easily. He didn't know how to put it, how to word it any better than he already had. "I'm worried."

"What about?"

"That maybe these powers aren't good. Why is it I can command forces of evil, but not forces of good?"

Derek raised his head upwards and gazed at the stars. Despite the occasional droplets of rain, it was a clear night, and the stars were dotted around the sky like a painting. There was so much out there, so much to explore, so much that they didn't even have the ability to understand yet. If they were so insignificant in the grand scheme of things, how were they to know the extent of Eddie's power, or the reason for it being there? But there was one thing Derek was sure of, one thing he could offer to reassure Eddie.

"It is not up to us to make sense of the world we are placed in, nor is it up to us to understand the gifts we have been given. It is only up to us to understand how we should use them." He turned to Eddie and looked him in the eyes, placing a reassuring hand on his shoulder. "One thing I do know, Eddie, is that there is not a bad bone in your body. You are a good person, and these powers are a part of you, so they must be good, too. Maybe you won't ever figure out what they are for, where they came from, or if you can even do what it is we all predict. But the one thing I can be sure of, is that whilst these powers are in your possession, they will be used for the forces of good. Because that's what you are. A grand, powerful, force of good."

Eddie was forced to smile, even blush. He looked to the ground and took in Derek's words. He was wrong to think that

Derek couldn't point him in the right direction or understand the path he needed to take.

"Thank you," he said sincerely.

They glanced back at the window of the house. The family were still in joyous tears, so they leant back on the bench and enjoyed another moment of triumphant silence.

OCTOBER, 2001

ONE YEAR, TEN MONTHS SINCE MILLENNIUM
NIGHT

CHAPTER FIVE

*K*elly couldn't hide the smile from her face as she danced across the kitchen, lost in a daze. She barely even noticed Mindy sitting at the table as she opened the fridge and pulled out a carton of fresh juice.

"Hey," came Mindy's voice, making Kelly jump. "So what are you so happy about?"

"Well, you know..." Kelly smiled and sauntered over to the table, pouring some juice into a tumbler. Her grin was stuck to her face.

"Ah, I see. Would the fact that you're wearing nothing but a man's shirt have anything to do with this?"

Kelly giggled, then suddenly felt self-conscious. She attempted to hide her legs, then realised she was too happy to care.

"Maybe..."

"And that it was your fifth date with Doug today and he came over to watch movies..."

She couldn't deny it. She had been taken with Doug since the day they'd met. Mindy and Kelly had become the best of friends, heading down to the student union bar for a drink and a gossip every lunch-time, then evening after lectures, without fail — and it was their Friday night out after the second week that she'd bumped into Doug at the bar and had recognised him instantly.

"Hi, it's Kelly, right?" He had smiled at her, and she abruptly became aware of every part of her body. Her arms instantly became too big, her knees gave way, and her hands just seemed to fidget around the label on her bottle of whatever it was she was drinking.

"Yeah..." He'd remembered her name! "And you're... Steven? Michael?" In her ridiculous stupor she somehow managed to make a joke. "Oh right, it's Nug."

Nug? she had thought, reprimanding herself. She had gone to say, "not Steven," and ended up going to say his name, Doug; and in doing so, had ended up saying both *not* and *Doug* together. She couldn't have felt more ridiculous.

"No, it's not 'nug.' Close, though."

Urgh! She had attempted to be cool, make a joke, (which she was sure would have been hilarious) and ended up making a complete tit of herself.

"No, I know it's nu — Doug," she replied, her voice cracking.

"Hey, how's about a dance?" he asked.

Oh God, a dance?

She loved dancing. Hell, she used to do dancing twice a week until she was eighteen and had to be sectioned. She did modern and hip hop. She had performed on stage many, many times, and had even gained awards for her dancing. Yet, somehow, she knew that if she attempted to walk out on that dance floor with this guy, who had a wonderful physique, fluffy spiked hair and a perfectly chiselled goatee, she knew that her knees would give way and she would look less like a dancing prodigy and more like an elephant with broken legs.

"Er, yeah, sure," she answered.

What the hell are you doing? her inner monologue continued. *You are going to make a complete idiot of yourself! He is way too cute to make an idiot of yourself in front of.*

Nevertheless, with the aid of a substantial amount of liquid courage, she paraded onto that dance floor and showed him how to move. He had been obviously impressed, pointing out how his dancing knowledge had been limited to "the dance of one foot to the other in time with the beat."

She grew more and more smug with how much she was impressing him, so smug that she stupidly attempted a turn — which would have been showing off way too much anyway — and landed on her ankle. Her legs had given way. She had fallen backwards into an incredibly smooth-dancing black guy, who had ended up spilling his beer, which landed all over Kelly's hair.

She could have died. Then and there, she didn't care. Someone could have come and taken her away to heaven; it would have been a lot better than the humiliation she felt. She was red-faced, drenched in beer that had soaked into her hair and made her stink, and nursing an ankle that was in a lot of pain.

She knew people were laughing at her. There was a circle growing around her of people sniggering and pointing. She hated herself. She wanted to cry.

That was, until Doug calmly knelt in front of her. He smiled that perfect smile of his and put his hand on her shoulder. At no point did he laugh, nor did he smirk or snigger or prod fun in anyway.

"Are you okay?" he asked.

Kelly just dropped her head to the floor. She didn't want to say no, as that would be such a blatant lie, but she didn't want to feign happiness when she was clearly distraught.

"Hey, let's get you a towel, dry you off, then I'll help you limp home. How's that?"

And he was as good as his word. He went to the bar and pestered them for a towel; after being told they didn't have one, he somehow convinced them to walk to the cleaner's closet and find a large cloth, the closest thing they had.

He took her outside; not in the back to the smoking area where everyone was gathered, but out front, further away from the building, beside a tree, away from where anyone could stare or point. He held her bag for her as she dried her hair, even helping as her arms got tired.

He helped her hobble home, his arm tucked securely around her waist, making sure there was no pressure on her ankle. He was a true gentleman, and his arm felt warm and secure around her, despite the dropping temperatures of the night air.

When he reached the door to her dorm, he did not try anything. He didn't make any jokes, nor was he persistent in trying to come in.

"Hey, once you're feeling better, it would be good to hang out. Maybe we should go for a drink or something," he had said. Then she'd replied, "Yov course" — something between "yes" and "of course." He left, letting her limp to her shower and shampoo the smell out of her hair again and again and again.

The first date that followed had been amazing. It was the best conversation she had ever had. She spoke about her parents, her family, how much she missed her cat, about why she chose to study psychology, how she wanted to work in mental health; the only thing she didn't tell him was where she'd spent her year off, which she didn't even consider for a moment. He was nice, but she didn't want to tell him she was strapped to a bed hearing voices for the better part of ten months.

He told her about how he was studying English Literature

as he hoped to go on to do his teacher training and work in a deprived area where he could help the kids who needed it.

He walked her back to her dorm again and kissed her. It was perfect; a full moon and a leisurely stroll, hand in hand with the perfect guy. It was the kind of kiss she could melt into — then he wished her good night and left.

After four weeks of dates, messages, and relaying every bit of information to her new best friend, Mindy, she plucked up the courage to ask him over to her room to watch a few movies. They were halfway through *Jumanji* when she turned and looked at him. He felt her gaze and returned the look, and when his eyes met hers, she could tell that was the moment.

Completely blanking out the movie, their kissing became more and more passionate, and before she knew it, she was unbuttoning his shirt and running her hands down his chest.

Then she lifted her head and inadvertently ruined the moment.

"This is only my second time, by the way," she blurted out. She hadn't considered what she hoped to achieve by shouting out such information, but for some reason, she just kept going. "I mean, I've done it more than once. Like, a few times. But with the same guy. And that was two years ago. And it wasn't very…"

He was simply laying there, smirking up at her. That's when she realised she had mounted him. He was shirtless and she was sitting atop him in her bra. The moment felt completely killed.

"Hey, no worries," he spoke in that tone of voice that always calmed her. "Look, if you think it's too fast, we don't have to. But I'm not expecting anything. I just really like you and I like where this is going."

His understanding in itself was such a turn-on. With a sneaky smile, she had resumed foreplay and they had made love far beyond the end credits of the film that still played on her television.

After they had laid there for an hour and he had begun to fall asleep, she had dressed herself in his shirt and left him snoring quietly to get some juice. And to tell Mindy, of course.

"Oh my God!" Mindy squealed. "I'm so happy for you. He is so delicious."

"He is," Kelly replied, her mind drifting back off to the clouds.

"So how was it?" Mindy sat forward, her face growing serious. "Tell me everything."

She smiled and fiddled her finger around the rim of her juice, staring at it absentmindedly.

"It was..." She tried to think of a word to describe it. "Perfect. Just how I thought it would be. He was so understanding, and he made sure I was happy with everything, and that it felt good, and... it was good."

Her and Mindy shared a smile that conveyed everything it needed to convey. Mindy, ecstatic for her friend, and Kelly having her head-in-the-clouds *Titanic* moment.

After a brief discussion with Mindy about some guy she was seeing who had turned out to be a dick, Kelly returned to bed. Being in halls of residence, they were forced to share a single bed, but this didn't bother her. She slotted herself under the covers beside him and his arm tucked itself around her. She laid there, just enjoying the closeness of his embrace until she eventually found herself drifting off.

She fell into a dreamless sleep at first. Then she started seeing images of her parents. They were taking her to the mental health clinic for the first time. She was seventeen. Her ex-boyfriend was there, as were a few of her teachers from school. She was sat in the middle of her room, surrounded by perfectly white walls, and they were all laughing at her.

"Kelly?" she heard. That's when her eyes opened. She

glanced at the clock in front of her. It was 5:38 a.m. Why on earth was she awake?

"Kelly?" came the whisper beside her.

"What?" she whispered, leaning her head around to peer at Doug. He was now facing the other way, and all she could see was the back of his head.

"Kelly?" she heard him whisper again.

She leant up, peering over at him. She still couldn't see his face, so she leant herself around him a bit more. Finally, she could see him. His breathing was heavy and his eyes were shut, evidently in a deep, deep sleep.

She frowned and looked around the rest of the room. Had she heard correctly? It was a light whisper, but she was sure she heard her name.

It could have been anything, she told herself. The wind, maybe. Except there wasn't any wind. A glance beneath the curtains behind the head of the bed showed her that the window was shut and the leaves of a nearby tree were motionless.

"Kelly?"

She turned her head around, staring wide-eyed at Doug.

Fast asleep. Not a movement. Breathing heavily.

She lay herself back down. She was imagining things, that's what it was. It was nothing. No one was whispering her name, no one was talking to her.

This is what happened before. You thought you heard something and they locked you away...

Except this time, she knew it was all in her head. She knew it wasn't real. She had probably just thought she had heard something. She was barely awake; she was not very aware and it could be anything making that noise and her mind was simply interpreting it as her name.

With that reassurance, she closed her eyes, drifting off into a silent, dreamless sleep.

CHAPTER SIX

Jason sat back in his chair with his coat neatly folded over his lap, stroking his beard. He felt old. He hadn't considered fifty-four to be 'old age,' but sat in this lecture theatre with numerous students more than half his age, he felt it. They were all so optimistic, bright-eyed and, unfortunately for them, gullible. Young people were always the most perceptible to fraudulent paranormal exploits, and he felt it was his duty to do them the service of saving them from being conned.

He flipped over the flyer in his hand.

Derek Lansdale, Professor of Parapsychology and Paranormal Science and author of 'The Truth about Exorcisms' performs a guest lecture at our university on Thursday morning.

How could he resist?

The lights dimmed slightly and the room hushed into silence. A man, possibly around ten years younger than him, made his way to the front with a spring in his step and a happy smile. He was immaculately dressed, with a waistcoat underneath a grey suit, his black tie done up, and his goatee neatly groomed. He gave the image of someone wise, someone people would listen to. It was all part of the act, as far as Jason was concerned. To be successfully deceptive, you need to look the part.

With a gadget in his hand, he pressed a button and a Power-Point was projected upon a large screen, showing a picture of him and two younger men.

"Good morning ladies and gentlemen, and thank you so much for being here," he began, confidently making eye contact with people around the room. "It is a pleasure to be here. Now, I imagine you could be divided into two sets of people. The first, believers; you know in your heart of hearts that the paranormal is true. Maybe you've witnessed it. Maybe you've been hurt by it. Or maybe you just can't deny the possibility. Then there are the rest of you. Sceptics. People who have come here to entertain the idea. To see what crazy nonsense I am going to come out with."

Jason glanced at the faces around him. Some people nodded, smiling to the person next to them in acknowledgement, already transfixed on the man.

"As you can see on the screen, this is my team. Eddie and Levi. And yes, those are their genuine names."

A few chuckles.

"Between us, we have attended upwards of sixty exorcisms. Each of them a tragic case of a demon inhabiting the body of its victim. These victims are typically young women, teenagers, or children, though we have come across numerous adult cases as well."

He removed his blazer and placed it on the back of a chair. He rolled up his sleeves, allowing a few moments of silence; a sign of authority, as Jason interpreted it. Command an audience by letting them know you are not scared to stop talking to gather your thoughts, not to be rushed.

"First thing we need to do when we attend a potential case is identify whether the victim needs spiritual or mental help. Not every case we attend requires an exorcism. In fact, I'd say less than two percent of people who believe themselves to be possessed are actually possessed. Quite often it will result in us saying to the parents, or family, that this person needs a doctor, not an exorcist. So how do we identify who needs our help and who doesn't?"

Derek clicked his gadget and the projection moved to the next slide, with the title *Unlearnt Skills*.

"There are numerous things we look out for, particularly things they could do that they couldn't do before. Such as the ability to speak in tongues. Latin in particular, as it is not a language spoken or used in modern age, is one to look out for — it is unlikely in this day and age a child would have picked up Latin from their friends at school. And with any other language, say French or Italian, we must look at that victim's past and ensure there is no-where else they could have attained that language from, directly or indirectly.

"Likewise, do they have any skillsets that seem unnatural for them? A six-year-old girl lifting a bed, perhaps. Speaking in more than one voice at a time."

He clicked onto the next slide. Jason took his reading glasses out of his pocket and put them on. The title of the slide read *Mental and Emotional Torment*.

"Fear, depression, voices, hearing voices no one else does, anger, rejection of other people, emotional breakdowns. Again, one needs to ensure these are not just mental health issues, so these symptoms would need to be alongside stronger symptoms also."

He clicked onto the next slide, reading *Abilities of the Unnatural and the Occult*.

"Does their skin burn and smoke on crosses and holy water? Sexual attraction toward animals – I was once confronted with a twelve-year-old girl who had sex with a pig on her family's farm." A few people groaned and flinched away. "Fighting ability, martial arts perhaps. Obsessions with pain, harsh words, rejecting the Bible."

He clicked onto another slide that read *Paranormal Ability*.

"And perhaps the most important, and definitive, identification of a demon being present. Do they have abilities that are beyond that of a human? Levitation in the air, telekinesis, throwing objects around the room that they are nowhere near, knowing things about complete strangers they couldn't have known before."

Derek acknowledged a young man with his hand up and pointed toward him.

"Yes?"

"So have you actually seen, like, some chick floating in the air?"

Derek chuckled to himself. "Well yes, as you have put it, we have seen a 'chick floating in the air.' Almost all the victims we have helped have levitated. It is a sure sign that their problems are not psychologically based. How many mental health victims, after all, do you know who have risen ten feet off the ground?"

Jason sighed. He was getting agitated. It was almost time. Enough of this man conning these young, impressionable people. They needed to be told the truth.

"In fact," Derek continued. "My colleague, Edward, has himself been risen off the ground. He has even been taken to the other side to confront the demon in Hell itself."

"Enough!" Jason bellowed, his declaration echoing against the walls. Every face abruptly turned and gawped at him. Derek instantly glared in Jason's direction. "Have you any videos of this? Any evidence of what you are claiming?"

"I do not have video evidence, I am afraid," Derek replied, his voice full of agitation. "We have tried a few times, but the video camera either lost its power or was destroyed by being thrown across the room."

"That's convenient, isn't it?" Jason said. "You're telling me, in this day and age, with the equipment you have available, the demons have somehow destroyed it?"

"I'm not sure what it is you are accusing me of, Mr...?"

"Aslan. Jason Aslan."

"... Mr Aslan. But I assure you, I do not lie."

"Then you don't lie and you're part of some self-induced group hallucination, that's fine. Maybe it's *you* that needs the mental help then, huh?"

Derek clicked his knuckles together, taking a moment to gather his thoughts. Half the room was staring at Jason, half at Derek. No one could move. The tension was unbearable. Derek contemplated his answer, taking his time, not being rushed by anyone, attempting to retain his authority.

"Mr Aslan, if you have any questions, I will be more than willing to answer them at the end. If you would like to have a conversation afterwards, I would more than happily oblige."

Jason rose, standing with his face in a snarl, jabbing his finger toward Derek.

"I will not be engaging you in any sort of question and answer session, thank you very much. I have spent my life debunking frauds like you, and not once have I come across someone who could provide me with the damndest bit of evidence. And you, sir, are no different."

"On the contrary, I assure you that if you came along to one of these exorcisms, you would be shown otherwise."

Jason laughed loudly. This man was persistent. Most would have run off stage bawling by now, with no counter-argument, guilty at being found out. Not this guy. This guy was stubborn.

"How can someone fund what you do? Have you subjected yourself to tests? A laboratory setting? Somewhere where all the extraneous variables can be controlled? Where we can ensure you aren't fooling us?"

"I'm not here for an argument about the integrity of-"

"Extraordinary claims require extraordinary evidence, Professor. And as far as I can see, all we have is your word."

"Mr Aslan, I'm afraid I'm going to have to ask you to leave."

Jason had no intention of staying, but he was not about to be removed on anybody else's terms. He gathered up his coat and made his way to the front of the auditorium, placing his belongings by the door. He strolled slowly to the front, alongside Derek, who scowled at him. Ignoring Derek, he turned and surveyed all the faces in the audience.

"Don't be fools, ladies and gentlemen," he told the congregation. "Don't let this man make you believe something because you want to believe it."

"Mr Aslan, I asked you to leave-"

"You are young, so you are a good group of people to con," Jason continued, completely ignoring the instructions to leave. "Don't let him."

With a large smile at the audience, and a blanking of Derek standing with his hands on his hips, he made his way to the door.

He made a point of stopping and taking his time in putting his coat on. Through one sleeve, then the other, then straightening up his collar and his sleeves. After ensuring that he had thoroughly aggravated the so-called paranormal expert, he made his way through the door and left.

CHAPTER SEVEN

"So, what are we doing here?" enquired Jenny, inquisitive yet hesitant. She was intrigued to see what Eddie could do, but at the same time cautious about meddling in what she didn't fully understand.

"Well," Eddie began, poised on the edge of her garden bench, then paused as a brief moment of nostalgia came over him. He remembered back to a few years ago, when he was a loser, an alcoholic, with no direction, and constantly tormented by grief over his sister's death; before he had even conceived of the gift he supposedly had. He'd lived on the sofa bed in the living room that led to this garden. He was exorcised on that sofa bed. He'd confronted many demons in there, both literally and metaphorically.

And now here he was. Sat with his best friend, his childhood confidant, his lifelong accomplice. Showing her what he could do. He felt proud that she was now in awe of him, considering how much of a burden he used to be on her.

"I have this gift," he continued. "Or so Derek tells me. I don't know."

"But you told me about that exorcism where you freed that

girl, right? You closed your eyes and saw the demon in her room from the car outside. How can you not think you have a gift?"

"Yeah, but I mean. I don't understand why. Or how. It's just so... confusing."

Jenny smiled sympathetically, nodding to show her understanding. He wasn't lying. There was so much pressure on him to make something of these powers.

"I need to find out what these powers are, what I can do. I need your help."

"And how can I help?"

"I need to try stuff on you. And I promise you won't get hurt."

She raised her eyebrows.

"I mean, I promise you won't get *badly* hurt."

"Fine," she sighed. She really was great — not many friends would agree to such a proposition with such little persuading. "What is it?"

He withdrew a screwed-up piece of paper with numerous scribbles on it.

"This is a spell, where I supposedly chant the incantation, whilst putting my hand on your chest, and if I am worthy — by that it means, like, if I have powers — then, supposedly, it will, I mean, probably, it will expel the demon."

"Okay."

"But, I mean, obviously, you don't have the demon. So it will just retrieve some of your energy, it will give me some kind of vision that shows you are clean."

"Clean?"

"Free of demons."

She took a deep, inward breath. Eddie could see she was wary, but at the same time, eager to help him. He was always able to rely on her, and he wouldn't have imagined asking anyone else in the world.

"Right, okay. What do I need to do?"

"Just, like, twist this way, lie down…"

He indicated for her to lay down on the bench. Gathering herself, mentally preparing, she turned and lay down.

"Okay, what now?"

"Just close your eyes."

She closed her eyes. She waited.

He psyched himself up; clenched his fists, shook his arms, nodded to himself, and began whispering, "Come on, come on, come on."

He knew not to put everything on this, not to invest all his belief in what he could do in this tiny moment, this first attempt. But, he was excited. He was sceptical. He wanted so much for it to be perfect.

He placed his hand over her heart and pressed, pushing down upon her. She gripped the side of the bench.

"Relax," he told her. She did.

He recalled the words in his mind. *Latin. Always bloody Latin.*

"De medio tollere, tolle de medio," he spoke at a slow pace and deep pitch, allowing each syllable to sound itself out. "Manum tuam et peccator."

Nothing.

He tried again.

"De medio tollere, toll de medio. Manum tuam et peccator."

His arm vibrated. He had a slight convulsion. She shook.

"De medio tollere, toll de medio. Manum tuam et peccator."

And just as it felt like the energy was flowing through his arm, was surging out of him, shaking her — it ceased.

All movements stopped.

The wind brushed against his face. He felt rain in the air.

Jenny's eyes stayed closed and her body stayed still. His body did nothing.

His face scrunched up in anguish.

"De medio tollere, toll de medio! Manum tuam et peccator!"

His screams echoed around the garden.

Nothing. Not a movement. Not a twitch.

Whatever had started happening was not happening. It hadn't worked.

With a sigh, he slumped down on the floor beside the bench.

"You can get up now, it hasn't worked."

Jenny opened her eyes. Readjusting to the light, she sat up, watching him, feeling his disappointment, recognising that familiar pout, the irritated sulk he would put on when things didn't go his way.

"We can try it again."

"No. I read it properly. It didn't…"

He bowed his head.

Maybe Derek's wrong. Maybe he's getting carried away. Maybe I'm getting carried away.

"You know this doesn't mean anything, Eddie."

He shook his head, bit his tongue, and looked away from her. He felt her hands stroking his hair and, before he knew it, she had slumped down next to him and taken his hand in hers.

"I know you had a lot pegged on this."

"Nah, it's fine, I mean-"

"Eddie. You don't need to pretend with me."

He closed his eyes. Wiped away tears even though there weren't any there. He looked at Jenny, who was looking at him with that soothing smile.

"We'll try again. Keep going."

He nodded and said nothing.

CHAPTER EIGHT

*K*elly spread out on the sofa, completely knackered. She had spent the last few weeks with Doug and had spent very little time away from her bed. The only real break she'd had from her bed was when they went to his bed. She was also aware of how cheap the bed was and, in all honesty, was becoming worried they were eventually going to break it.

She attempted to lift her text book to do some studying. She had an assignment due in a week, but her heart wasn't in it. It was on 'theories of conditioning in advanced therapy,' but she was both tired and dubious. She had experienced these therapies and illnesses; the people setting the assignments evidently hadn't. She'd had people try to treat her through conditioning, attempting to create an engrained feeling on her through repetition. If anything, it had just made her angrier at those imposing the treatment on her.

Every time she tried reading books about these techniques, her mind drifted off to bad places, unforgiving recollections and distressing images. Ultimately, her treatment had backfired, as it conditioned her to feel worse and worse the more she thought about it.

But still, if she ever planned to help people in her way, she needed to get the qualification to do it. Even if it meant playing along with the bullshit they preached to her.

They'd never had mental health issues, they had only studied it. That was the problem. They had no idea what it was like.

"Hey, Kelly," Mindy greeted her as she sauntered into the living area and clicked on the kettle. She had a huge smile, as always; Kelly wasn't sure how she did it, but she was always happy.

"Hey, Mindy, how's things?"

"Wonderful. And you? No Doug tonight?"

She grinned at the mention of his name. She couldn't help it.

"No, we're having a rest day today. I think we have gotten to the point of exhaustion."

"You're telling me. I'm in the next room, remember."

Mindy smirked at Kelly, who rolled her eyes playfully and smiled back. Mindy took her cup of tea and ambled over to the sitting area, curling up on the sofa and cupping her mug.

"I don't even care," Kelly joked, giggling at her. "We are having such a great time."

"That's awesome. He seems like a really nice guy."

"So what about you? I saw a guy leaving your room the other day."

Mindy practically snorted into her cup of tea and shook her head.

"No, no, just a bit of fun. We can't all commit ourselves so young as you have."

Kelly raised her eyebrows and turned her head away. A fair point; she was a one-man woman, no doubt about it. Mindy was not, and she had no problem with that. She was young and she was enjoying herself.

"So I heard you knocking on my wall last night by the way, sorry I ignored you."

"What?" Mindy looked puzzled.

"Last night. You were knocking on my wall at, like, eleven. I assumed you wanted to watch a movie or go for a drink or something, but I just fancied an early night."

"I didn't knock on your wall, Kelly."

How odd, Kelly thought. She could swear she had heard three audible knocks against her wall. Maybe it was Mindy knocking her bed against the wall, or dropping something.

"Besides," Mindy added. "I wasn't even here last night, I was with that guy. Adam, I think his name was."

* * *

KELLY LAY asleep in her bed, curled up with the duvet wrapped around her. Her room was cold, as she couldn't figure out the radiator, but beneath her duvet she was toasty warm.

She spread herself out as she turned over. Having shared a bed every day for the past few weeks, it was liberating to have the whole space to herself, allowing her to spread her body out and soak up the space. As nice as it was, she would still have preferred to have Doug beside her.

Knock, knock, knock.

Her eyes opened. She glanced at the clock. 3:01 a.m. Who was banging on her door at this time?

Knock, knock, knock.

She slowly pushed her duvet down and twisted herself out of bed. She wrapped her arms around herself. Despite wearing two layers of pyjamas, she still felt the icy cold in her room.

She rotated the lock and lifted the door handle, withdrawing the door backwards to plant her eyes upon...

Nothing.

No one.

An empty doorway.

She leant her head out of the doorway and peered back and forth. The lights of the hallway came on; they were motion sensor lights and they lit up the corridor, to reveal no one, and a row of shut doors beside hers.

If someone was knocking on my door, then how were the lights off?

She shook her head to herself, thought nothing of it, and closed the door. She locked it and walked swiftly back to her bed. Just as she started to climb back into bed, she heard it again.

Knock, knock, knock.

She leapt back out of bed and stormed toward the door, turning the lock and swinging it open.

Nothing. No one.

She left her room and knocked on the door next to hers.

"Mindy? Mindy, that you?"

No answer. She knocked again, but heard no movement inside. She assumed she wasn't in and was shacked up with some other guy again. Either that, or she was fast asleep in her bed, oblivious to the world.

She returned to her room and shut the door behind her, locking it. She hesitated. Kept her ear against the wall. Listening out for... well, she wasn't sure. But she knew what she had heard.

This was how it had started before. Sounds like this. Knocking on the door. Someone whispering her name. She had sworn it was real, without a second thought to what it could be.

But this time it was different. This time she was aware that she was hearing things. She could tell it wasn't real, it was just in her mind. She wasn't going back to how she was.

Back then, she had no idea it was all in her head, but she did now.

Or was it?

Because she had heard three clear knocks against her door. She knew she had.

Once a few minutes of silence had passed, she edged back to her bed. Whoever — or whatever — it was, had clearly left. Or her imagination had ended its hallucinations. One or the other. Either way, it was late, and she wanted to get enough sleep to be able to stay awake in her morning lecture.

She returned to bed and pulled the duvet tightly around her. She curled into a ball and enjoyed the comfort of the bed. In her cocoon, she was warm, relaxed, protected.

She closed her eyes and drifted off. Her mind relaxed and she let go of all the things that had happened to her in the past year. She was over it now.

It was done.

She was resting.

"Kelly."

She sat up with a start. Switched on the lamp beside her. She spun herself in a full rotation, scrutinising every part of the room; every angle, every corner, every crevasse. Someone had said her name. She had heard it, clear as she had heard the knocks.

But no one was there. It was just her.

"Hello?" she offered, not entirely sure what she was expecting.

No one answered. No one responded.

Of course no one responded. There was no one there. She was completely alone.

She laid back down and brought the duvet back around her. It was her mind, all in her head. A tired brain playing tricks on her. A slight relapse to how she had spent the last year of her life. Bad feelings resurfacing, that was all. Nothing more.

She felt suddenly cold. She lifted her head and looked down. Her duvet was halfway down her, settling on her waist. She was sure she had wrapped it around her. She knew she had.

It must have slipped down.

She reached out to pull it back and in one swift movement the duvet dragged itself to her feet.

She was paralysed. Her eyes as wide as they could go, frozen in a stare at her bare feet beside the duvet. Had she just seen that?

The duvet just slid down of its own accord.

She wasn't going back. She couldn't. Not now. Not after she had done so well; she had a best friend, she had assignments, an amazing boyfriend — she could not slip back to old ways. She wasn't going back. She was not returning to a mental health unit. Not again. Not ever.

It was her mind, same as it always had been. She was seeing things.

Or maybe it was a breeze that took it away?

Her bare ankles had goosepimples, her arm hair stuck up. She couldn't tell if it was coldness or terror, but she could feel a frozen brush of wind against her.

Where is that wind coming from?

She double checked; her window was securely shut. The door was locked. There was no way wind could get in.

She opened the desk drawer and withdrew a packet of medication. She rifled through it, the packet shaking in her trembling hands.

She popped a few pills and shoved them into her mouth. She swallowed them dry; she had taken enough pills that she didn't need water to wash them down anymore.

That medication was there for emergencies. That's what the doctors had told her. It was there if old feelings resurfaced. They would calm her down, help her sleep.

She laid down, leaving the duvet where it was. She would go cold tonight. She was not prepared to let the duvet be dragged away by her own imagination again.

Within minutes her medication had taken effect and she was unconscious. The next morning, she made a deal to not speak of this to anyone.

She would not go back.

JANUARY, 2000

TWO DAYS SINCE MILLENNIUM NIGHT

CHAPTER NINE

*E*ddie sipped on his coffee, feeling its comfort against his dry throat.

He felt wrong. Something had severely disturbed him, and he could not explain why.

"We are so, so grateful," assured Beatrice, her arm around her daughter, Adeline. Eddie had spent his New Millennium night battling the three-headed demon Balam from her body.

There were so many questions. For starters, what was a demon the stature of Balam doing possessing a regular, insignificant girl? This was not some everyday demon, some servant of the devil, like the demons that normally attacked the victims Eddie was used to helping. This was a great and powerful king of Hell, commanding over forty legions of demons.

Why would a ruler of demons possess a girl? Why would he lower himself to something that was so far beneath him that it surely couldn't give him any pleasure?

More pertinently, why had this demon taken his own sister hostage? His sister, who had died when she was a child, had spent years and years suffering in Hell at Balam's hand. Sure,

Eddie had freed this girl, had freed his sister, had removed Balam from this world. But he wanted more. He wanted Balam, this despicable prince of hell, to suffer.

"It's quite all right," Eddie spoke distantly, distracted by his thoughts.

"I wish there was something we could give you," Beatrice whimpered. "We just don't have much in the way of money or possessions…"

"It's honestly okay. I do this because it is my duty, not because I am after some kind of reward."

And the demon, the way it had responded to him… He had let it take his body so he could battle it remotely, but it had seemed shocked to see him. Like it knew him.

"It is you," Balam had spoken. "Commander of hell, he who attempts to take his throne."

Attempts to take *his* throne? Who exactly is *his*? Whose throne is Eddie trying to take?

Eddie was a good, honest person, who took it upon himself to use the power he had been bestowed with to fight hell's demons.

He had no choice in having this 'gift,' as Derek constantly referred to it.

"You have no choice in having this gift," he heard Derek's words echo in his mind. "But you do have a choice what you do with it."

"If there is ever anything we can do for you," Beatrice continued, "please know that I will forever be in your debt."

"That honestly will not be necessary," Eddie answered and finished his coffee. "I must be leaving now."

With a nod, he walked to the door. He was stopped by Adeline, the young, innocent girl he had battled to save, who rushed up to him and grabbed his hand.

She reached her hand out and opened it. In it was some sort of craft, something she had evidently made herself.

"This is a friendship bracelet," she told him, her voice so innocent compared to the foul, predatory bastard that had been speaking out of her mouth the night before. "I made it for you."

He smiled. His thoughts were elsewhere, and he wasn't used to receiving gifts, but he took it gratefully. He ruffled her hair and gave her a faint nod in appreciation.

As he left the house, he closed the door behind him and walked to the end of the street where Derek was waiting. Eddie kept the friendship bracelet in his hand, staring down at it.

"Where's your car?" Eddie asked, wondering how Derek had gotten there.

"Remember Levi?" Derek replied. How could Eddie not? Levi had assisted Derek on his own exorcism. He had gone off and done his own thing now, but Eddie was still grateful for his help.

"Of course, why?"

"Well," Derek said, smirking. "He has a role on a ghost hunting show, and they have given him his own helicopter."

"No way!" Eddie said, both astounded and a little jealous. Good for him.

Derek pointed beyond a few sets of trees in the distance and, sure enough, Eddie could see the rotor blades of a helicopter.

They both walked toward the rotor blades and their conversation turned to the exorcism Eddie had just performed.

"How did it go?" Derek enquired.

"I… don't know. I got rid of it," Eddie said absentmindedly, still distracted. He pocketed the sweet gift the girl had given him and turned to his mentor.

"I'm sorry I couldn't be there for this one."

"Ah, it's okay. Though the demon was more big-time than we are used to. Ever heard of Balam?"

Derek's eyes grew in shock.

"Surely not!" he said. "It must have been lying. It was claiming to be what it was not, you can't be sure."

"I can. I saw it in its true form. Three heads, one of a human, one of a bull, one of a ram."

Derek took a moment to let the news sink in. Balam? Possessing a girl? Why?

"He said some things as well. Things that I don't understand. Derek, who am I? Why do I have these powers?"

"I told you-"

"It said I was the commander of hell. It said I attempted to take 'his' throne. It said it will return with armies and take me down."

Derek nodded, stroking his goatee, staring into the distance, deep in thought. Eddie knew him well enough to know he was struggling for an answer or explanation. He would always attempt to help, but maybe this time, this was beyond even his understanding.

They walked beyond the clearing and approached the helicopter. Levi leant against it, in his tattered jeans and scruffy goatee. Eddie and Levi exchanged a nod. Eddie wished he could say more, but his mind was dwelling too much on the situation at hand.

"Derek, is there any way these powers aren't powers of good? That these haven't been given to me by Heaven, but by Hell?"

"Nonsense, how could that be? You have done so much good with them."

"But there must be a reason these powers make demons scared. Seriously, what am I? Why am I really here?"

Derek opened his mouth and found that nothing came out. These were very good questions, ones that Derek couldn't get beyond hypothesising with. There were theories, yes, but they weren't panning out.

Maybe Eddie was right. Maybe it was time to start entertaining the idea that this gift may not in fact be a gift, but a curse. Maybe it was time to consider whether Eddie was sent here as a force for good.

"I think we need to come up with some possibilities," he offered.

"You've come up with so many, Derek, and none of them-"

"No, I've been hiding from the obvious. I've just been looking at the good options. You're right. Maybe it's time we start looking at possible reasons that aren't as favourable. Maybe we should look at ways that your powers could be used for reasons less than honest."

He had pushed Derek to this point, Eddie knew that. He had prodded him to look at this possibility. But he had never actually heard Derek admit it, never mind say it aloud. Coming from his mouth, it felt a lot worse.

They were going to have to hypothesise that maybe Eddie wasn't here for the right reasons.

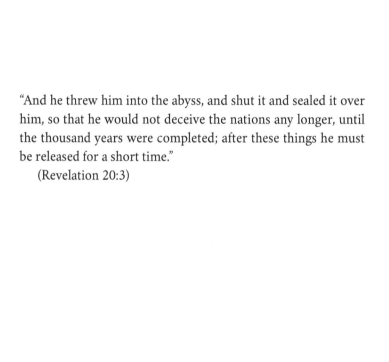

"And he threw him into the abyss, and shut it and sealed it over him, so that he would not deceive the nations any longer, until the thousand years were completed; after these things he must be released for a short time."

(Revelation 20:3)

NOVEMBER, 2001

ONE YEAR, ELEVEN MONTHS SINCE MILLENNIUM
NIGHT

CHAPTER TEN

*K*elly caught a glance at the photograph on her bedside table. In it was herself, her mother, and her father. Except this was from before. Before she had been sectioned, before they had coerced her into admitting she was 'unhinged' as they called it.

She tried to ignore it. Doug was beneath her, gazing up at her body, wide-eyed.

He always seemed to look so amazed every time he saw her naked. His eyebrows would go up, his eyes would alight and his mouth would start flickering.

It made her feel special, the fact that he found her so attractive, when she considered him to be so out of her league.

She closed her eyes, forced all bad thoughts out of her mind and enjoyed the moment. She was moving her hips back and forth in a way Doug had shown her to. It didn't bother her too much that he was vastly more sexually experienced than her, as he knew what they needed to do to have great sex. And it was great sex, she could not deny it.

She felt him inside her, moving back and forth. Her hips were pressed down as she rocked her backside, her clitoris pressed against his body, rubbing against his skin. She moaned unknowingly, reeling from the pleasure.

She opened her eyes and looked back down at him. He met her gaze and smiled. He lifted his head back and groaned, moving himself further inside her every time her hips moved forward.

She caught sight of the picture again. Why the hell was this picture distracting her so much? Was it because it was from a time so different to who she was now?

Then, suddenly, she realised something she was yet to think of.

Her scars.

She had quite a few of them, up the inside of her thigh and across her back; she had been a prolific self-harmer, so much so she had to be restrained by doctors numerous times.

Had Doug seen them?

He must have.

He had gone down on her numerous times and kissed her inner-thigh; there was no way he could not have seen them.

And when he had sex with her from behind, her in ecstasy on all fours, had he been looking at them then? Thinking about them as he penetrated her? Wondering where they were from?

Either he was ridiculously unobservant and hadn't noticed, or he had noticed and had chosen to say nothing. What did that mean?

Stop it! she told herself.

He was looking up at her, with a pleasured face, but also a slight bit of worry, like he was noticing her distraction. Like he could tell her mind was elsewhere.

She buried it all away in the back of her mind and smiled down at him. She took his hands in hers and placed them upon her breasts. His grin grew as he grabbed them. She loved it when he grabbed her. It made her feel so... passionate. So intense, like he had to have her.

It spurred her on.

She forgot about everything.

She focused on nothing but the fervent grasping of her skin in his hands, the feel of herself rubbing upon him, the deepness of him; it filled her with tingles and she felt like she was about to burst.

Her legs shook, her breathing quickened pace, her moaning grew more frequent. She could feel it. She was close.

In the corner of her eye, she saw the photograph.

Forget about the fucking photograph, she willed herself, and continued, on the precipice of pleasure.

That's when, at the cusp of orgasm, in a final glance at the photograph, it changed.

Her face was rotting. In the photograph, she could see her face peeling off, her skin turning dead, foam filling her mouth, blood dripping off her teeth…

The eyes moved.

The eyes of her face in the photograph, she saw them move.

They looked dead on hers, transfixed.

She could feel Doug slow down beneath her.

"Kelly!" the face screamed from the photograph.

Kelly shrieked and threw herself onto the floor. Doug sat up and looked down at her, completely taken aback. Kelly didn't even notice.

She grabbed the photograph and threw it across the room. The frame cracked and the glass shattered to pieces. She didn't realise what she had done until she looked up, shaking in the corner of the room.

Doug was stood, backing away, the duvet tucked around his waist. He looked terrified, his arm cautiously reaching out toward her, as if trying to assure a rabid animal that you meant it no harm.

"Doug…" she whimpered. "Help me…" Tears were lashing

down her cheeks. She was freezing. Her body was shaking out of horror and she needed Doug now more than ever.

Without hesitation, Doug put some underwear on, no doubt feeling self-conscious about his nudity, and took the duvet to Kelly, wrapping it around her. He sat next to her, tightly tucking his arms around her and rocking her back and forth. He kissed her gently on the forehead.

"It's going to be okay..." he whispered.

"Doug..." she sobbed. "Have you seen my scars? On my legs? My back?"

Doug bowed his head and closed his eyes, then lifted his head back up and gazed at her.

"Is that what this is about?"

Kelly shook her head. She didn't know what this was about. What was she supposed to say? That she saw her face rot and shout her name in a bloody photograph? It was ridiculous, she knew it.

"Can you get me my medication? It's in my desk drawer."

Doug nodded slowly, as if he was just taking in that she had requested medication, something he clearly had no knowledge of. He took the packet out and glanced at the name of the drug, passing it on to Kelly.

"Kelly?" he said, watching her pop the pills and swallow them down whole. "This medication is called chlorpromazine. That sounds pretty, I don't know..."

She handed him the packet and he placed it back in her drawer. As he did, he sifted through some of the other medication.

"Haloperidol, Loxapine... Kelly, my aunt had a breakdown and this is the kind of... this is antipsychotic medication."

She didn't know what to say. He was staring at her, his eyes demanding answers. She reluctantly stared back. Where would she even start? Did she want to even start? Was this something she wanted to tell him? Ever?

"I… I had a breakdown."

"This looks like more than a breakdown, Kelly. Why don't you tell me what happened?"

He took her hand and slowly guided her back to the bed. He leant against the wall and put his arm around her, allowing her head to rest on his chest. She stared at a space on the floor below her and didn't take her eyes away from it.

"I'm not going anywhere," Doug told her. And she believed him. She truly believed he was not leaving and she felt secure in his arms. She had to tell him. She had to get it out in the open, otherwise he would think she didn't trust him. And she knew he would need to know at some point. Though she hadn't accepted it, she knew.

She spilled everything. From the start, how it had begun, who was there, what she did.

January 2000, it had started. Almost as soon as the new millennium had arrived, so did the voices. Telling her she was worthless. Telling her she was going to kill everyone. She remembered standing there as her family sang "Auld Lang Syne," with their waving arms crossed as she collapsed to the floor, knocking over the table holding the champagne and smashing the bottle everywhere.

"Everyone you love. All of them. You are going to kill them." It kept repeating it over and over. "You will kill them. Kill them. Kill them. Kill them."

She had clambered through the hallway. Her hands were bleeding from propping herself upon carpet covered in broken glass from the champagne bottle she had inadvertently shattered. She left smears of red on the doors and the walls as she used them to prop herself up. She ended up in the kitchen, her mother following her. The last thing she remembered from that night was vomiting. When she awoke the next day around mid-afternoon, her mother informed her that she had attacked her grandmother with a piece of broken glass.

She had no knowledge of it whatsoever.

February 2000. She stole a knife from the supermarket and used it to cut herself; to begin with, on her thighs, then on her lower back. She knew she was doing it. She stared down at the knife in her hands as she drew blood, but she felt nothing. Not physically or mentally. It was as if she wasn't in control.

Everywhere she went, she heard whispers, like people she couldn't see were saying things in her ears. Like they followed her around everywhere, but she couldn't see them. She'd been in a clothes store, buying a blouse, and they would tell her, "You could kill that woman." She'd stare at the lady asking her if she wanted a receipt and they'd tell her, "You could wrap that blouse around her neck and squeeze it until she suffocates." Only she would hear it. No one else. And she would do everything she could to resist.

March 2000. She woke up half way through the night in a trance. "Take the knife. Your mum is asleep." She dragged her feet through the hallway. Next thing she knew her dad was restraining her against the wall and her mother was crying, clutching a wound upon her chest. She didn't have time to apologise or check if her mother was all right, she didn't even have a chance to say that she loved her; she was locked in the garage, unable to get out.

That's when they sectioned her.

April 2000. It was humiliating. They would leave her in her room all day. It barely met the minimum standards of living. Everything was white; the walls, the bed sheets, the furniture. She was told on her induction that white means they can't hide anything. Any blood or substance would show up. There were no secret corners in this facility.

She couldn't have many things because they were a danger to her. She had to be supervised when brushing her teeth, as they were scared she would use the toothbrush as a weapon.

She wasn't allowed mouthwash, as she could use it to poison herself.

She was on great terms with one of the wardens, and even played chess with him a few times. The warden would sneak her extra puddings in the tray of disgusting food he was forced to deliver. He would take her to the television room and supervise her after his shift had finished, just so she could have some time away from her room and avoid cabin fever.

That stopped when she woke up one day on top of him. She was naked, with part of a tray that had somehow been carved into a razor held above her, the warden cowering beneath her. She had no idea when she had taken off her clothes, or even created such a weapon. But she was restrained to the bed for the rest of the night nonetheless.

"They are trying to hurt you," the voices would tell her. She would scream and lash out as much as she could, fighting against her restraints. Above her she would see a red cloud with the faces of people she loved.

May 2000. She was denied visiting rights. Her parents could only communicate with her via phone. She was deemed as too much of a risk to be let out of solitary confinement.

She felt like she should be in prison. She would have more freedom than being trapped in this place that made her stir crazy. The environment was conducive to her needs.

June 2000. She figured out she needed to stop being honest. Stop telling her psychiatrist that she heard voices. She told her they were going away. She told her she was feeling better in herself. She told her she no longer felt a risk to herself or anyone else.

July 2000. Somehow it became a self-fulfilling prophecy. The voices stopped. The attacks stopped. She was released from solitary confinement and her privileges were restored.

August 2000. Her parents saw her for the first time. She cried in her mother's arms. She apologised and apologised. She told her mother she loved her and would never want to hurt her. She didn't know what happened, as she had blacked out, but she would never knowingly hurt her. Her mother cried also. Her dad remained strong. Their relationship began to repair.

September 2000. No issues.

October 2000. They decreased her medication.

November 2000. They announced her release.

Then December came and she returned home for Christmas.

What she did not tell Doug, however, is what happened on her release. As she stood in the doorway, her parents signing the release forms, breathing in the outside air for the first time in ten months, it started again.

The voice returned, but only for a moment. It said:

"The greatest trick the devil ever played, was convincing the world that it did not exist."

It was a lot for Doug to take in, she knew. She didn't know what kind of reaction she expected. She just expected one. But she got nothing. Doug sat in stone-cold silence, staring ahead of him. She watched him uncomfortably for as long as she could stand, until she had to break the silence.

"Well? Please say something, Doug."

He nodded to himself, then turned and met her gaze.

"It's a lot to take in. I mean, it sounds like you've been through a lot."

"Does it freak you out?"

"Well, yeah, a little bit. I'm not going to lie."

She closed her eyes and bowed her head, instantly regretting everything she had just revealed.

"But hey," he said, lifting her chin up so she looked at him. "All of this contributed to you being the woman you are today. And that is a woman I care about deeply. So it's a lot to sink in, but..."

He shrugged his shoulders and forced a smile at her. She knew this was the best she could get. She had just told him a lot and it must be quite a shock.

"Okay." She smiled at him and they laid down together. He put his arm around her and she closed her eyes.

They didn't say another word for the rest of the night.

FEBRUARY, 2000

ONE MONTH SINCE MILLENNIUM NIGHT

CHAPTER ELEVEN

*E*ddie sat alone in the corner of a dimly lit pub, sipping on a pint of lager, then placing it carefully on a coaster. He had a bag of books and papers from the university propped up against the seat beside him. He looked around at the other customers in the pub, then withdrew the first book and placed it on the table. He had managed to seclude away from anyone else and was pleased he was not attracting any attention.

He opened *Demonology: Tricks of the Demons* and scanned the contents. He wasn't entirely sure what he was looking for, but he'd know when he found it. He knew not to let what demons say to him during an exorcism get to him, but he couldn't help it. Too many times they had taunted him with words of encouragement for him to embrace a supposed evil side. Too many times they had said, "It is you." They had attempted to provoke him and he had wielded power over them so easily, far easier than Derek ever could, and he had grown to be one of the most powerful exorcists in the world in such a little amount of time.

In the contents was a chapter entitled *Verbal Taunts.* He

picked out the page number and flicked the pages along until he found it.

Demons are frequently known to be aware of history and personal information about those around them. They consistently use this against their victims. Many times, a dead relative, a distant partner, or even insecurities that had never left your mind, can be picked up on and used against you.

HE KNEW THIS ALREADY. He wasn't arguing with it; he'd learnt far more about Derek's personal life from what demons had said than what Derek had said. It was just not what he was looking for.

Sure, demons may have been saying this stuff to taunt him. Like Derek had said, maybe his powers could be used for good or bad, and they were simply trying to tempt him. It just didn't feel right. It felt like something more.

He withdrew the next book. The Satanic Bible. He had read passages from this before and it had not been what he expected. It hadn't been all about praising the devil, but instead giving the opposing view to Christianity and backing it up with rationality.

When a Satanist commits a wrong, he realises that it is natural to make a mistake — and if he is truly sorry about what he had done, he will learn from it and take care not to do the same thing again. If he is not honestly sorry about what he has done, and knows he will do the same thing over and over, he has no business confessing and asking forgiveness in the first place.

EDDIE WAS TAKEN ABACK as to how much this made sense to him. As opposed to the black-and-white views of the Bible, dictating what is wrong and what isn't wrong, this simply explained realistic human emotions rationally and bluntly.

He turned to another passage.

Satanism has been frequently misinterpreted as 'devil worship,' when in fact it constitutes a clear rejection of all forms of worship as a desirable component of the personality.

THIS MADE COMPLETE SENSE. Although he fought demons, and despite being in Hell for a small period of time, he would still dispute the origin of the monsters he fought. He said prayers and cast out demons with God's name, but he never applied the ethics and morals of any form of Christianity to his life, because he disagreed with so many of them as a foundation for how you should live. He found that none of them left any room for the varied perspectives that inevitably exist. Every event has multiple points of view, and it is humans that have invented the concept of deciding one of them is wrong and one of them is right.

He slammed the book closed and swiped it away from him. What was he doing? Reading the Satanic Bible and agreeing with it? He had devoted his life to ridding the world of the demons that represented this book, now he was relating to it?

He stood up. He wasn't sure why, he just needed to be on his feet. He needed to go somewhere. Do something away from going around in circles with research. Circles that led him to sympathise with a representation of evil.

Scooping all the books back into his bag, he downed the rest of his pint and threw the bag over his shoulder. Without making eye contact with anyone, he stormed out of the pub and to his car that was parked down the road.

He dumped the bag in the boot and marched to the driver's seat — then froze. In the distance, he could see a church. He was intrigued. How would a place of religion react to him?

Would it accept him now as it always had?

Locking the car door without taking his eyes off the religious building before him, he gormlessly trudged toward it, bumping into a few people on the way without even reacting.

He stepped into the church and left the daylight. It was dark, with the dank shadows of the stone structure and grand stained-glass windows surrounding him. It had that damp smell in the air that churches often had and he could feel the moisture against his face and in his nose.

He walked forward and instantly felt a stabbing pain in his chest, a pain alike to indigestion or heartburn. He grabbed hold of his torso and pressed his hand against his chest.

He took another step forward, and a shot went through his stomach. A twisting, agonising feeling went through him that he couldn't explain.

Adjusting himself to the pain, he made his way through the middle of the pews and to the front of the church.

He propped himself up against the font, peering into the holy water. He saw his reflection waving in the water. The sound of a priest approaching distracted him for a moment. He waved his hand over the water and nothing happened. He didn't know what he was expecting, but nothing happened.

"Can I help you?" asked a priest to the side of him. Eddie ignored him, not even glancing to see what he looked like.

He dropped his hand lower and lower, gently placing it upon the water's surface. He quickly withdrew it with sudden pain and fell to his knees, clutching his wrist.

The palm of his hand was completely red, a sizzling cloud of smoke exuding from it. He clutched his wrist, not daring to touch his hand in fear of the pain it may cause.

The priest knelt beside him and looked upon his hand, the smell of burning flesh filling the air between them.

"Son," he addressed Eddie, slowly and calmly. "I think you need to leave."

Eddie looked to him with eyes of terror, the priest's words going straight over his head. He had just burnt his hand on holy water. How? Why?

After realising he had been asked to go, he stood and strode out without argument, still clutching his wrist, not taking his eyes off it.

As he left the church, the pain in his chest and stomach ceased and his palm began to heal.

CHAPTER TWELVE

*D*erek paced back and forth in his office. His hands furiously fidgeted and he was sweating profusely. He had never felt this agitated before. Of all the things he had faced, this was the biggest one.

He decided to check it again. It must be wrong. There must be something about it that was wrong.

Then again, it was just a book. Just a book written by some idiot somewhere who didn't know what they were on about. Just because something was written in a book doesn't make it real. Just because someone wants to substantiate their claims by making money out of them, does it give it integrity? No!

He sat at the edge of his seat, took the book back out of his drawer, and slammed it on his desk. He ran his hand over the top, wiping away some of the dust that covered the title: *Prophecies of the 21st and 22nd Century*, by Bandile Thato.

Such a rare book itself, he was privileged to have it; bestowed on him in the early 1990s by Bandile Thato himself, one of only three copies he'd produced. A gift for freeing his wife from demons. It was all luck that he was in South Africa at the time and met him. At least that's what

Derek thought, but Bandile insisted there was no such thing as luck, and that his being there was no coincidence. He had kept this book for so long, locked in a safe where it could do no harm.

Bandile called it a gift. Derek saw it as a curse. He did not want the knowledge as to what evil incidents were going happen in the world, as there was no way he could prevent them. Knowing such things only caused him pain when he had to witness such events.

But it was still just a book. Written by a man. A wise man, yes, but a man with eyes that could see the future... preposterous, right?

Still, the book did have many prophecies that had proven to have some value.

Some value? Who was he kidding? Every prophecy in that book had come to pass. Everything. Every act of evil, every terrible event. Political changes that Derek could have had no impact on whatsoever. Russia was to have an unexpected new president, 113 dying in Concorde crash in Europe... it was all there. Written clearly and precisely for him to read.

He had even glanced at a few of the upcoming prophecies from time to time, the most prolific predicting the death of 2,996 people on 11 September 2001. Then he would do all he could to erase it from his mind, knowing if he was to toy with the timeline of the future, even to avoid catastrophic events, it would be to meddle with powers far beyond his reckoning.

He rushed through the pages, returning to the prophecy that had caused him such alarm.

And there it was, on the 666th page. He read it again, slower, making sure to have comprehended it thoroughly. He had read it so many times already, but reading it once more made him hopeful that somehow the words could be interpreted in a different way.

They couldn't. Its words and the implication were undeniably consistent with his interpretation of the last time he had read it; and the time before that, and the time before that...

There will be a man with powers to command demons in hell. There will be a man with powers to exorcise a demon from its prey with ease that others do not have.

Come the new millennium, the world will hail the arrival of the first coming of Hell. The son of the devil. He will embrace the world and his powers will control all demons that stand in his way.

This will be the man with such power, and the son of the devil's coming will begin through him on 1st January 2000.

In this time, the son of the devil will carry through its ascension. Fate will align the son of the devil with its God, and the man it has chosen will give way to his true fate.

Come the new millennium, the son of the devil will rise and his powers will take him.

HE DIDN'T BLINK. He didn't move. Every word was the same as the time before and he couldn't interpret it any other way.

But what of Eddie? So he had some powers, what did that matter? His powers may have become stronger since the new millennium, but they were two months into the new year and he was in no way the devil in human form. Sure, this prophecy may be true, but why be so certain it was about Eddie?

He bowed his head, allowing it to drop onto the table. He wished he had never encountered this book. He wished it had fallen into someone else's hands. He wished this predicament did not lie before him.

Was the only way to stop this to kill the son of the devil? Would death make the evil end, or would it just provoke the beast within? So many questions he couldn't answer, so many things he wished to know. Most of all, why did this dilemma have to fall before him?

He stood and began pacing again, feeling his legs grow weary from the burden placed upon them. He paused at the window and looked outside. It was growing dark. He observed the students walking past. All of them going about their business, unaware of the realities of this world, perhaps going for a drink or having some tea. Oblivious to what stronger people must do to allow them to live out their ignorant, unknowing lives.

The candle on his desk flickered. That happened so often he ignored it. There was no breeze, no open window or ajar door to cause it to flicker, but still it flickered. It had flickered ever since he had started his work ten-odd years ago.

Then it came to him. His only solution. He must hide the book. Keep it locked away where no one would know. Even better, he would burn it.

He wasn't burying his head in the sand, he was just denying the possibility. If Eddie was not to know of his power and its true origin, he could continue living out his life, using his power for good. Surely it would only be the knowledge of this potential fate that would sway him in such a direction that he would be forced to become the successor to Hell.

He picked up the heavy book. It was old and tattered, in weak condition, which would help him well. With only a moment's hesitation, he ripped all the pages from the inside of the book.

He emptied the contents of the bin over the floor and placed it in the middle of the room. He grabbed all the pieces of ripped paper in his arms and chucked them in. He watched them for a moment, taking the spare candle in his other hand, and considered the implications. The people he could have helped with this book. The fates he could have been aware of. Could he have even prevented any of them?

No. Knowing what was in this book did nothing but burden him. He did not need it.

He dropped the candle into the bin and the papers went up in flames. As he watched them flicker and disintegrate, he ripped apart the leather cover and threw it into the fire piece by piece.

Eventually, the book was gone and all that was left of it was ash. He swept the rubbish back into the bin on top of the residue and placed the bin back in the corner of the room.

He left his office, locking the door behind him, leaving with it his knowledge of what lay in store for Eddie.

NOVEMBER, 2001

ONE YEAR, ELEVEN MONTHS SINCE MILLENNIUM
NIGHT

CHAPTER THIRTEEN

*J*ason barely made it one step through the door before he was thrown onto his back by two enthusiastic grandchildren. He laughed playfully as he dropped his bag and lay on the floor, with them climbing on top of him.

"Jesus, you're getting heavy…" he moaned beneath two small girls: Ava, aged five with long, brown, swiggly hair, and Mia, aged three, with bright-blond hair and a smile that would make your knees melt.

"Come on girls, off Grandpa," came the voice of their mother, Jason's twenty-four-year old daughter, Harper. "You know his knees can't handle it."

"Maybe if you both were to help me up — take one hand each, you can manage it!" He reached his hands out so Ava and Mia could take one each and tug as hard as they could. Jason feigned a struggle and made his way back to his knees.

He gave his wife, Linda, a kiss, then sat down on the stairs to take his shoes off.

"So what have you two been up to today?" Jason asked his two granddaughters.

"We went down to the park!" shouted Mia. She had only just managed to put coherent sentences together and already she wouldn't shut up. Just like her mother. "And I went on the swings."

"The swings?" Jason repeated with amazement. "How lovely."

"And I went to the sweet-shop," interrupted Ava. "And Nanny bought me some liquorish!"

"Some liquorish?" Jason choked back his laughter at the attempt to say *liquorice*. "I bet your daddy is going to love that," he said, with full knowledge that their father was a dentist.

"Yeah, well maybe some things we don't tell him," retorted Harper, leaning in the doorway, remembering all the times she used to come home and tell her father the things that she had done while he'd been away.

He regretted how much of an absentee father he had been at times, but his work had been important. He was lucky that he had managed to travel the world, debunking fraudulent mediums, psychics, and exorcisms in whatever corner of earth would have him. There was even a summer where the government became fascinated with the subject, quite a few decades ago now, and sent him to do scientific testing whilst sworn under deadly secrecy.

Those days were long gone. He had published enough books on the matter that his television appearances and lectures, combined with his best-selling non-fiction literature, would keep his family afloat. Now he was able to concentrate on being a wonderful husband and the all-time greatest grandfather.

He hadn't long settled into his favourite chair with a cup of tea brought to him by his loving wife — two sugars, just a drop of milk, the way only she could make it — when he was pounced upon again by two girls holding out a book, demanding that he read to them.

"You two are old enough yourself to read now, aren't you?"

"Yes, Grandpa, but we want you to read it!" Ava adamantly answered back. He gave in. He couldn't hold out against these girls, his caring for them was too strong.

He opened the book and began reading. Some story about a rabbit who did something or other. Not before long, there were two sleeping girls on his lap, snoozing away in his arms.

As he looked upon the two gorgeous girls cuddled up to him, peacefully sleeping and gently snoring, two precious gems, he looked to his daughter. She was deep in conversation with her mother across the room. She was a great mum. He was proud.

He thought back to his mum, remembering how she was. Cold, unloving, foolish. He was put in foster care before he was even a teenager, solely because of the kind of con artists he had since dedicated his life to opposing.

He remembered watching her leave the house for the last time, painfully hoping she would return soon, but knowing in the pit of his stomach he would never see her again. His tearful eyes peering out the window at an old man with a beard, shoving her into his car. He didn't understand who he was, what he was doing, until he was much older, and his solemn grandparents told him.

When he was an adult, he would come to learn that this man was the leader of a religious cult. An expert in brainwashing. A man who physically and emotionally abused those he supposedly led.

The cult leader was arrested when Jason was seventeen, for inciting many of his followers to commit suicide as proof of their love for God. Jason had always dreamt of seeing his mum again, but by then it was too late. She had already been conned. She had already died for this man.

He swore he would never let anyone face the same fate as her again.

The evening grew dark and it was time for his two angels to go, so he carried them out to Harper's car and placed them carefully in their car seats. With a kiss on their foreheads and a whisper of "Love yuh kid," he waved good-bye to his daughter as she took the two sparks of his life home to bed.

That left him and his wife alone to enjoy each other's company beside the fire. They had a television, but they rarely had it on. He preferred to spend his time caught up in a book, or learn how to check his emails; something that still took him over half an hour to figure out each time.

Linda had made his favourite for tea — shepherd's pie. He ate it quickly and it made her smile. Something as simple as how eagerly he gobbled down her cooking, even after all this time, still made her happy.

They sat together on the sofa, holding hands, as she read her magazine and he read his book. Eventually, the night grew late and she announced that she was off to bed. He told her that he'd join her later, gave her a kiss, and reminded her that he loved her, just as he had done every other day of their life, and was left alone.

Being sat alone with your thoughts is a dangerous thing. They would often dwell on the worst. Not with Jason. He knew that anything that worried him could be put down to a rational trail of thought and for that reason, he was never disappointed to be stuck in his own company.

He made his way over to the pad by the telephone. After all this time, his devoted wife still wrote down each message for him with such precision that every bit of detail about the call was recorded. She had noted one message, written as so, beneath a meticulously written phone number:

Time: 1.05 p.m.

    Derek Lansdale, from the university, head of Paranormal Science

Phone back

HE RACKED his brain to think of who this was, then it hit him. The man from a few weeks ago, the guest lecturer. Ringing up to give him a piece of his mind, perhaps. Wouldn't be the first time. People who place their beliefs on such weak foundations and deny evidence always react in a volatile way when those foundations are shaken. He discarded the message and went about his day.

Then, as if by bizarre coincidence, the phone rang, and Jason picked it up.

"Hello?"

"Good evening, I do apologise to call so late. Is that Mr Aslan?"

Jason frowned. Who the hell could this be? He glanced at the clock. It was gone eleven. It was late.

"This is, and who am I talking to?"

"You may well remember me, my name is Derek, Derek Lansdale — I gave the lecture that you protested against a few weeks ago."

"Ah, yes. I got your message. I'm not interested in hearing any abuse you have for me, and I request you do not call me at home, so-"

"Oh, on the contrary, Mr Aslan, I am calling to do no such thing. I always respect someone who is willing to stand up for what they believe in. I imagine you would too?"

Jason was taken aback. He didn't know what to say. It took him a few seconds of stuttering over his words until he could coherently reply.

"Well, yes, but I think it depends what those beliefs are based upon."

"Ah, well, what if I was to tell you that I have evidence for those beliefs that you contradict."

"I've seen evidence and it hasn't matched up, I'm afraid."

"Well, yes, I'm sure, but I am not talking about evidence such as you have seen before. This is not some bad cold reader doing readings, nor is it some man with an ear piece predicting people's past as it is fed to them. This is hard evidence you cannot argue with."

"Oh yeah?"

"I'm not talking someone just speaking in tongues in a way that could be otherwise explained, Mr Aslan. I am talking about a child floating ten feet in the air. I am talking about objects flying around the room. I am talking about being in the presence of things that are unlike anything you will have ever seen in your entire career. Mr Aslan, this is the real deal."

Jason couldn't deny that he was intrigued. He had heard all this diatribe before from numerous hacks who had set up tricks to make someone shake a bed whilst having a seizure, who had planted things around the room that made things jump in the air. But this sounded like a man desperate to prove something.

"You have my attention."

"In a few weeks' time, me and my partner, Edward King, are performing an exorcism of an eleven-year-old boy. I would like to invite you to come along. To observe."

Jason opened the curtains and surveyed the field outside. He enjoyed the stillness and the quiet of the night.

"I have no intention of watching some trickery, I assure you. I have seen objects flying across a room, and I have explained how the frauds did it afterwards."

"Mr Aslan, if you can explain how these objects fly across the room in some other way, then I would happily bend down and call you my new messiah. I would even let you bring in a video camera, if you wish. Then, you will either have footage of another hack, and will prove me wrong and end my career — or you will have footage of a genuine exorcism, and you will have had a shock like you have never had in your entire life."

Jason stroked his chin. He couldn't resist an opportunity like this, another instance of proving someone wrong. And this man seemed so adamant, it would be pure triumph to take him down a peg or two.

"Okay, I agree to your terms. I will attend this exorcism."

"Wonderful, Mr Aslan, excellent news. I will have the details sent on to you."

"Okay."

"Thank you ever so much, and good night."

"Good night."

He placed the phone back in its place on the window sill and watched the still night out the window. The trees, the grass, the beautiful night sky. So many wonderful things in this life, why do people keep needing to convince themselves there's more, when this life we have is already so blessed?

He finished off his evening with a glass of whiskey and made his way upstairs to bed. With a wash and a careful brush of his teeth, he climbed in next to his wife, tucking his arm around her and sleeping soundly.

CHAPTER FOURTEEN

Kelly prodded at her roast dinner with her fork. She'd been so hungry all day, but as soon as she had seen her parents, she'd lost her appetite. And now here she was, sat across from them at the carvery just down the road from her halls of residence, Doug sat beside her making polite conversation with her dad.

"So what is it you do for a living?" Doug asked, taking a small mouthful of beef.

"Well, I own a company that specialises in sporting products."

"Sounds fascinating."

"It's really not," her dad chuckled. "But it's nice of you to say."

"Kelly said that you are studying English Literature," her mother said, taking a sip of her red wine.

"Yes, I hope to do teacher training afterwards and teach English."

"Oh, how wonderful. You obviously have a lot more ambition than Kelly does. You are quite the catch."

Kelly scowled at her mum. She couldn't tell if it was a genuine dig at her, or whether her mum actually thought that little of her own daughter. Either way, she didn't meet Kelly's eyes, so she couldn't tell.

She had been feeling sick every time she had thought about this meal over the past few days. Doug had had to calm her down numerous times. She practically threw up last night when she fully remembered her parents were coming to visit.

Why am I so afraid of my stupid parents coming to see me? she thought, feeling frustrated with herself. Maybe it was because they were there when she broke down. They were there when she was sectioned. In fact, they were instrumental in getting her sectioned and put away in a mental health clinic with as much stubbornness as she had ever seen from them.

Now, here they were. She had cleaned up her life. She had laid down the foundations for a stronger future. She even had an amazing boyfriend who was too good to be true. And the whole time she felt like her parents were still judging her, like it wouldn't be good enough. Like she still needed to prove something to them.

She just wanted them to know her life was no longer a complete disaster.

"Are you okay Kelly?" her mother asked, turning to her. "You've barely touched your meal."

It was true. Kelly had been prodding it with her fork for the last ten minutes and had only taken around three or four mouthfuls.

"Yeah, I'm fine," she lied.

"So, how are... you know. Things?" her mother asked, and instantly her father and Doug went silent. Their eating slowed down and they stared at the table, avoiding eye contact with anyone.

"Fine, Mum," she answered, stressing the *f* and the *n* of the word *fine*. She realised this was indicating the contrary to what she had just said, but hoped that her reaction would provoke no further conversation about it.

"So my lectures are fascinating," Kelly said, changing the topic. "We've been doing one on conditioning, and the use of it in therapy."

"Oh, like you had?"

"Please, Mum-" She stopped herself mid-sentence. She didn't want to keep referring to it. She desperately wanted to move on. Her parents hadn't seen her for three months, so perhaps they couldn't recognise the change she had made that she was so proud of.

They shared a few moments of silence.

"Kelly?"

"What?" She whipped her head up, glaring at everyone around the table. They glanced at each other with confusion etched over their faces.

"Kelly, we didn't say anything," her father answered.

She looked around the table. No one had said her name. She had heard it, but no one had said it. She dropped her head to her food again.

"Kelly, you there?"

She lifted her head again and looked around the table. Everyone had their heads down, eating their meal. No one had said anything.

She glanced over her shoulder. There was nobody near them. A few people at the bar maybe, but not close enough to be able to say something without everyone else hearing it too.

That's when she noticed a man at the bar. A grey-haired man with a long beard, sipping on a pint of ale. She didn't know what it was about him, but something intrigued her. Her eyes transfixed on him.

That's when he turned his head and looked at her. His face

dripped. Literally, his eyes fell and turned to smoosh. His eyebrows trickled down his face and merged with his sagging mouth, creating one singular piece of mess on his head. His skin trickled onto his clothes, on his lap, his face turning to droplets.

She closed her eyes and shook her head, squeezing her eyes shut, willing her mind to straighten up. She opened them and looked to the man once more.

He was fine. Just sitting there, sipping on his pint of ale, completely unaware of the young lady staring at him.

"You okay?" Doug whispered to her.

"Yeah, fine," she snapped, and turned back to her meal. She could feel her parents staring at her, but she ignored it. She shovelled food into her mouth to give the image she was fine, anything that would stop their concerned looks.

"You should kill them," came the deep voice again.

She ignored it. Carried on eating. It was all in her head. Can't let her parents see her like this. Can't let them know that there was anything unusual about her mind, whatever the cost.

She would not go back again. She would not leave the life she had made for herself — a best friend, a boyfriend, a degree that was going well. She would not leave it, not for anything. Even if that meant lying to her parents.

Even if that meant lying to herself.

"So tell us about the town, what's that like?" her mother directed at Kelly.

"Erm, it's nice…"

"They deserve to die."

"… Within walking distance…"

"And you know it."

"… Good shops…"

"They locked you up."

"People are friendly, say hello to you."

"Do not ignore me you fucking bitch."

She closed her eyes and bowed her head. She leant her elbows on the table and ran her hands through her hair.

"Are you all right?"

"I need to go to the bathroom."

Kelly threw her napkin from her lap onto the table and scarpered to the bathroom. She barged in and marched straight to a sink, bowing her head and closing her eyes.

She ran the hot tap and splashed the water over her face. She kept soaking and soaking herself until she finally shook herself out of it.

She looked in the mirror.

A man stood behind her.

She spun around.

Nothing. No one. Not a soul in the bathroom with her.

It was just her, alone.

She turned back to the mirror. He was still there behind her, watching her, out of focus. She glanced over her shoulder again and saw nothing, but when she turned her head back he was still there. Unmoved. Unaltered.

"What do you want?"

"I will never go away, Kelly. I am not a trick of the mind. I am a trick of your soul. I have latched myself onto you and you may as well embrace it."

"Please, just leave me alone."

"I am in you, Kelly. I am not psychosis. I am real."

"*Fuck off!*" she screamed at her reflection, tears streaming down her cheeks, punching the mirror numerous times. She implored it to leave her alone. So she could be normal. So her mind could be healthy.

She heard a gentle banging on the door. "Kelly?" came Doug's voice.

"I'm in here."

Doug entered and was immediately taken aback by the sight of Kelly. He ran up to her and took her in his arms, squeezing her tightly against his chest. He shushed her and stroked her hair. He told her everything would be all right.

He told her she would be fine.

CHAPTER FIFTEEN

*E*ddie felt warm inside. It had been a while since he had managed to find time to have lunch with Jenny and Lacy, but sitting with them in the coffee shop, sipping on a cappuccino, the time in which they hadn't seen each other felt insignificant.

They had been instrumental in his transition from the washed-up alcoholic sleeping on their sofa bed to the university lecturer and successful exorcist that he had become. Jenny was his oldest friend, having known him since they were born. She was there when his sister died, she was there when he attempted suicide six years ago and now, she was there, in the happier times. She was there to enjoy the success of what Eddie had become.

"So then we got to the top of the hill," she continued her story, she and Lacy in hysterics, Eddie unable to help but smile along. "And she forgot her bloody camera. All that time, desperate to get a picture on top of the hill, and she forget the camera!"

Lacy gave Jenny a gentle nudge, playing at being offended, but all the while smirking along.

"Man, I can't believe how long it's been since I hung out with you guys," Eddie said, still smiling.

"I know," Jenny agreed. "And to think I used to see you every day on our sofa bed."

"The other day I saw her gazing at it, with eyes all over-come," Lacy said, and Jenny shoved her jokingly. "She missed you being there, however much she would complain."

"Oh, it was incessant, wasn't it?" Eddie joked. "'When are you going to move out,' like, every day."

"And now here you are. Who'd have thought it, huh?"

Eddie bowed his head and blushed. He fiddled with his mug in his hands. It meant so much that they were proud of him. They were the only family he had left.

"So what's it like, anyway?" Jenny asked, calming the laughter. "Being a world-renowned exorcist?"

"I don't know if I'm world-renowned…"

"Please, you are so renowned. Like, all over the world."

"I can't even do that damn spell," Eddie said, thinking back to Jenny lying on her garden bench, bracing herself for an impact that never happened.

"You will."

"I don't know, I just… I don't know." Eddie was pleased she had faith in him, but he had tried that spell on both her and Lacy numerous times since, with no effect.

"Whether it works or not, think of how many people you have freed, how many people you have helped. You have done more than enough to deserve the title of world-renowned."

Eddie smiled. It was nice that they thought a lot of what he did. Especially as Jenny had been such a sceptic at first.

He thought back to when Derek had to perform an exor-cism to rid Eddie of a demon. She had been vocal in removing Derek from her house and, when she finally let him back in, it was too late for him to help. Luckily, Eddie had managed to find a way by crossing over and facing the demon that was attempting to steal his place on earth himself.

For so long now, he had assumed that place was Hell. He had never considered it beyond that assumption. Both he and Derek had agreed that that was what it was, without ever actually discussing it.

"We're working on a young boy at the moment. Derek is setting up an exorcism for in a few weeks. We're taking some sceptic with us, Jason Aslan, or something."

"Jason Aslan?" Jenny repeated. "I've heard of him. Yeah, he's like a big-time debunker of frauds; he's been doing it for years. I'd be careful of him. He could hurt your reputation quite badly."

"Except that we're not frauds. So, once he sees what we can do, he'll be convinced."

"Unless he believes he can give another explanation to it. I'd be careful."

"Yeah, well it's Derek he's going against anyway, so, it's his bed, isn't it?"

Eddie noticed a dog at the next table over staring at him. It sat, not blinking, not moving, its eyes completely transfixed. He shifted uncomfortably and decided to ignore it. Whatever, it was just a dog.

"So how's your job going nowadays?" Eddie asked Lacy, trying to keep his attention away from the mutt.

"Oh, I'm just a nurse, never mind me. Ask Jenny."

"Okay," Eddie chuckled. "How's your job, Jenny?"

"Okay. I don't know, not really sure it's what I want to do."

"What do you mean?"

"I worked at a publisher because I wanted to be a writer. I just spend all my time reading over other people's stuff."

"Then why don't you write some stuff? Get it seen by your boss. You're in the best position."

The dog growled. Eddie couldn't help but look back at it, as the growling was so sinister and prolonged it was becoming unavoidable.

"What is it?" Jenny asked, and she and Lacy turned to look at the dog.

"Stupid dog won't stop staring at me."

Its growls grew angrier and it bared its teeth. It had a clear dislike of Eddie and it wanted to show it. It had no intention of looking away, it just remained poised, baring its teeth, incessantly snarling.

"Just ignore it, Eddie."

Easier said than done when the thing was obsessed. Before he could complain any further, it started barking at him in between growls. Again and again. *Snarl, bark, snarl.* Non-stop.

"It's doing my head in." Eddie leant his head against his hand, turning away from the dog, trying to put a barrier up that would keep him away.

But the dog wouldn't stop. It just kept barking and growling. It even started howling, too. With every sound it made, it grew more aggressive.

"Shut up." Eddie turned to the dog. He looked to the owner, who was completely distracted by a conversation she was having with someone else. How could someone be so oblivious when the dog was making so much noise?

It continued. More and more, louder and louder, angrier and angrier.

"Shut up, for fuck sake."

"Eddie, calm down."

Louder, angrier, bigger, it snarled and snarled.

"*Shut up!*" Eddie screamed, turning to the dog and looking it straight in the eyes.

Without warning or explanation, the dog went up in flames. Everyone leapt out of their seats and backed away. The owner of the dog fell to her knees and cried out, but her friend dragged her away.

It wasn't just a small flame; the dog combusted into a huge ball of fire. Its howling ceased and its frantic struggling grew slower, until the flames engulfed a body that lay on the floor.

Jenny stared at Eddie. Saw the look in his eyes. It didn't seem to cross Lacy's mind, but Eddie could feel Jenny staring at him. Like somehow he had done it. Like somehow, he was responsible.

A waiter ran out with a fire extinguisher and put the fire out. It took a good while of spraying, but after an anxious wait, the flames went. The owner dived upon her dog in uncontrollable tears, crying over its blackened, burnt, dead body.

Eddie just stared. The carcass laying before him. No idea what had happened. No inkling as to how he could explain it.

Well, no explanation he wanted to entertain anyway.

DECEMBER, 2001

CHAPTER SIXTEEN

*D*erek and Eddie stood together, tentatively watching Jason pull up in his car.

"You know, this could totally backfire," Eddie said.

Derek nodded.

"I heard from Levi today," Derek announced, attempting to dwell their minds on other things. "Remember him?"

Eddie nodded. Levi had both assisted on his own exorcism, and choppered them away from his confrontation with Balam. He had graduated with first-class honours and was now working on some ghost hunting television show. They were pleased for him, though missed his presence; he had always been a great help in Eddie's early days with Derek.

"He owes me a favour," Derek smirked, "and he's only down the road today, I'll get him to chopper us out if need be."

Eddie briefly laughed, ending his humour quickly as Jason approached.

Derek stepped forward and shook Jason's hand firmly. Eddie stepped forward, shook Jason's hand, and retreated behind Derek. He wasn't as forthcoming, and was unwilling to show feigned pleasure at Jason's presence. He performed better without a judging audience.

Derek stood back to allow Jason a thorough look upon the house they were about to enter. It was a small, semi-detached house on a rural council estate. It was grey, with roots running up it and cracks in the walls. In all honesty, it wasn't a great sight to look at.

Derek perched himself against the fence outside the house and invited Jason to do the same. Eddie did not come closer. He remained leant against the car, eyeballing Jason from a safe distance.

"I suppose your first question," Derek began, "is how on earth did we determine that this boy is possessed?"

"Yes. How are you not sure the help this boy needs is psychiatric, rather than spiritual?"

"A very good question." Derek smiled at Jason, gesticulating enthusiastically with his hands. He was clearly excited to prove to the great sceptic, once and for all, that demons did exist.

Eddie was not so eager. He leant back with his arms folded and his eyebrows sunk into a frown.

"You see, Mr Aslan-"

"Call me Jason."

"Very well, Jason. You see, the majority of these cases we are invited to, I would say around ninety-eight percent, we determine that there is nothing of 'spooky' origin whatsoever, and we advise the family to take the victim to a psychiatrist. We must go through a rigorous testing process before deciding on such an extreme decision so as to perform an exorcism."

"And what is this rigorous testing process?"

"You attended the lecture, Jason, you must surely remember. This boy's bed shook whilst he was completely still, objects moved of their own accord. He even spoke another language."

Jason sighed. "Speaking another language is not necessarily sign of a ghost. You don't know where he picked up that language, you don't know what he sees on TV or hears at school."

"It's a demon, not a ghost. And, I'm afraid you don't quite understand."

"What don't I understand?"

"Well, this language he was speaking. It was not French, or Italian, it was Akkadian."

Jason looked confused. He tried to think of where he might have heard that language before, but couldn't. He shifted slightly and turned back to Derek.

"I don't know that language."

"Well, no, you wouldn't, would you?" Derek smiled. "Because it doesn't exist anymore. It was used around 2000 BC, in ancient Mesopotamia, which today would probably be Iraq or Kuwait. Can't think of any television programs to feature that."

Derek stepped toward the front door. Eddie couldn't help but feel a little smug as he followed Jason along the short path to the house surrounded by overgrown grass and dead flowers.

Derek stopped before he knocked on the door and turned to Jason.

"Oh, I almost forgot. There are a few health and safety issues I need you to abide by." He looked Jason dead in the eyes. "Number one, you do not move from your spot in the room. Number two, you do exactly as I tell you at all times, without question. Number three, and possibly the most important — whatever it does, or says, you do not talk to it. Ever."

"Got it."

"I'm being serious, Mr Aslan. You may not believe it yet, but what we are dealing with is pure evil, demons straight from hell. Do you understand?"

"Clear as day."

Derek knocked on the door. Jason glanced over his shoulder at Eddie, as if wanting someone to exchange an amused look with, but got no such reaction. He prepared his video camera and followed Derek into the house.

Jane Abbot, the mother of the boy, shook Derek's hands, followed by Jason and Eddie. She was overweight, with curly hair and a bright-red face. She wore clothes as if she was a repressed housewife in the 1940s. Every item in the house was covered, either by plastic cloth or fastened by duct tape.

"Mrs Abbot, it's good to see you," Derek greeted her.

"Yes, thank you so much for coming."

"My pleasure. Do you mind if we come in?"

She nodded timidly and welcomed them in, as Derek introduced Jason and Eddie as his partners.

"It's nice to meet you all. Thank you so much for coming."

"Mrs Abbot," Jason interrupted. "Can I just ask — why is the furniture either covered or fastened down?"

She looked at the furniture and fiddled with the apron loosely tied around her waist. "I just had to. Everything that was loose just kept flying about the place."

"And taping them down has stopped it?"

"No, to be honest with you. It hasn't."

She led them into the living room, fetching them each a cup of tea as they perched on the edge of the sofa.

"How is Billy?" Derek asked. Almost as if prompted, a loud bang and a morbid scream shuddered the ceiling above them.

Mrs Abbot took that as a sufficient reply and forced a sad smile, avoiding eye contact with anyone.

"Are you planning on filming this?" she directed at Jason.

"Yes," he answered. "If it is all right with you?"

"What's it for?"

"Oh, just for me. As a record."

She nodded loosely, vacantly, her mind somewhere else.

"Please relax," Derek comforted her. "We are the real deal. We will help your son. I promise." He smiled at her and she smiled back her first genuine smile of the evening so far.

Derek stood and placed his cup of tea down. "Do you mind if we go up?"

"Of course."

He placed a reassuring hand on her arm and gave her the faintest of nods. He went up the stairs slowly, looking around himself, followed by Jason then Eddie. The walls were void of pictures, now just a series of vacant hooks going up the stairs; presumably taken down because of the boy.

The floor-boards creaked beneath them as they approached the room with caution. Derek slowly placed his hand on the door handle, pushed it down ever so slightly, and opened the door as carefully as he could.

It was freezing. Despite the hallway and the downstairs being toasty and warm, this room made them shiver as soon as they set foot over the threshold. Jason glanced back at Eddie, who hadn't even registered the coldness. Eddie was used to this.

Derek approached the bed where a boy lay asleep. He pointed to the far side of the room and instructed Jason to stand there as Eddie took his place next to Derek.

Jason took out his video camera and began filming, standing in the place he had been instructed to stand.

Derek put his hand on the boy's shoulder and gave him a gentle nudge. The boy stirred and looked up at Derek with groggy eyes.

"Billy, my name is Derek," he told him in a quiet, comforting voice. "This is Eddie, and behind me is Jason. Can you tell me, please, Billy, is this you that I'm talking to?"

Staring up weakly, the boy faintly nodded his head.

"Thank you, Billy, you're doing brilliantly. Can you tell me, are you alone in there?"

With a glance at Eddie and Jason, who were gazing back, awaiting his answer, he looked back at Derek and faintly shook his head.

"No. Thank you, Billy. This thing in there with you. It's hurting you, am I right?"

Billy's eyes welled up. He didn't nod or shake his head this time; instead, a tear fell from his eye.

"Okay, thank you, Billy, you've done really well. This is Eddie." He lifted his hand to point to Eddie behind him. "He is going to get the demon out of you, and I am going to help. Do you understand?"

Billy nodded.

"This means we are going to have to provoke the demon to reveal itself. Which means you are going to have to be really brave for me. Is that okay?"

Billy nodded and closed his eyes, bracing himself.

"You've done really well, Billy, well done."

Derek nodded at Eddie and took his place across the room.

Jason watched in awe, undecided about what he thought about the whole event, staring at Eddie kneeling next to the child and opening his palm. He moved his hand above the child's head in circular motions.

"In the name and by the power of our Lord, Jesus Christ, demon reveal yourself," he whispered, so faintly Jason could barely hear it.

"Demon, be snatched away and driven by the church of God and from the souls made to the image and likeness of God. Demon, you will be not redeemed by the precious blood of the Divine Lamb."

The boy's chest rose and pulsated. The boy's eyes had closed and his body flopped, all apart from his chest, which rose and sunk in repetitive motions.

"Most cunning serpent, reveal yourself."

The boy's body trembled violently.

Jason's eyes widened. He glanced at Derek and turned back to Eddie knelt over the boy. Was this a fit? Was he not going to do anything about this? Why was a doctor not present?

"You shall no more dare to deceive the human race, persecute the Church, torment God's elect, and sift them as wheat. You will reveal yourself."

The boy's twitching grew furious. His whole body shook. Foam gathered in his mouth and Eddie rose to his feet, keeping his hand out over the boy, moving faster and faster in circular motions.

"The most high God commands you, demon, show yourself!"

Jason couldn't believe what he was seeing. Billy was in a full, uncontrollable seizure and they were doing nothing. He needed urgent medical help; people could swallow their tongue and choke, or end up with irreparable brain damage should they strike their head on something. He needed to do something. He needed to stop it somehow.

"He, with whom, in your great insolence, you still claim to be equal. He commands you. Demon, *I* command you, show yourself!"

"Stop!" Jason cried out, desperately rooted to the spot.

"Quiet," demanded Derek, adamant nothing would interrupt Eddie, knowing that bringing forth the demon was a crucial part.

"He's having a seizure, he needs help!" Jason cried out.

"Jason, Mr Aslan – please be patient. Once the demon is present, you will have your evidence."

"He could die!"

The boy's fit had become uncontrollably ferocious. His head hurled back and forth, narrowly hitting a full strike against the headboard behind him. Eddie just stood over him, repeatedly shouting for the demon to show itself.

Jason had to do something. He couldn't let this go on.

Without a second thought, he lurched forward toward Eddie. Derek stood in the way and stopped him, pushing him back up against the wall.

"What are you doing?" Derek demanded.

"Can't you see? This boy needs serious help."

"Yes, I can see, and that is why you must not interfere. Do as I instruct."

Jason pushed Derek off him and heaved himself out of the room, slamming the door behind him. Derek decided not to go after him. What was happening in that room was more important.

Almost as soon as Jason had stormed away, the boy's seizure concluded and he lay still. His body leisurely rose into mid-air and halted. Deep, croaky breathing filled the room.

Derek burst open the door and looked for Jason. "Mr Aslan, you might want to get in here!"

It was no good. Wherever he had gone, it was not there. It was a shame he would not be able to prove the existence of a demon to him, after all that he'd had to grit his teeth through, but this was more important. The demon had surfaced. This was Eddie's opportunity to vanquish it.

"Demon, tell me your name," Eddie commanded.

The demon simply grinned. Eddie was used to this. They all started out so cocky. So full of themselves. He loved destroying that arrogance.

The demon sluggishly twisted its head and looked at Eddie with a piercing glare — then its eyes widened. A face of overwhelming astonishment and pleasure came over it.

"It is you," it directed at Eddie. "It is true. You have risen."

Eddie glanced at Derek. Derek said nothing. He had buried the prophecy for almost a year, and it hadn't come up since. He had hoped that would be it. That it was done. Evidently not.

"It's just playing with you, Eddie," Derek decided. "Don't let it."

"It was said you would rise come the new millennium," the demon persisted, happy and bewildered. "And here you are. I am at your mercy. Tell me what your bidding is and I will do it."

Eddie just stared back. Astounded, shocked, confused, unable to make sense of what the demon was on about.

"I want you to leave this boy's body. Find another to torment."

"As you wish."

The boy's body trundled off the bed with a thud. Eddie knelt beside him and checked his pulse. He glimpsed over his shoulder to Derek, who stood there in as much surprise as he was.

"It's a trick, surely?" Eddie perpetuated. "He can't have gone that easily, that just doesn't happen."

"I don't know, Eddie," answered Derek. And he really didn't.

"His pulse is fine," Eddie observed, then moved his hand to the boy's forehead. "His temperature's gone back to normal. How could a demon have obeyed me so easily?"

They weren't able to conjecture for long, as the door burst open and a horde of men erupted into the room. Jason led the crusade, followed by two men wearing matching jackets and Mrs Abbot thrashing out at them. The two men barged their way to Billy, urgently checking his pulse and temperature.

As this point, the boy screeched in anguish, his yelps mixed with furious mirth and belligerent cheers.

It was a trick. The demon hadn't gone anywhere.

"What the hell is going on?" Derek addressed Jason.

"I called social services," Jason answered. "They needed to know."

"You complete and utter fool! I invite you to observe a genuine piece of evidence and this is what you do?"

"The boy was having a seizure."

"The fucking boy was possessed!"

With a skirmish and a quarrel that involved the boy's mother thrashing and fighting out repeatedly, desperately resisting the invading men, social services took Billy downstairs and the mother ran after him.

Derek and Jason stood there, in a stand-off, both as disgusted as the other. Eddie joined Derek's side, focused on Jason with utter disbelief.

"Do you know what you have done?" Eddie said.

"Yes. I have saved a young boy from delusional abuse. And I will be making the university aware of the kind of things you are doing to young children. You can expect to be facing the dire consequences of this very, very soon."

Eddie and Derek clasped their hands over their open mouths in stunned silence.

Then it hit Eddie smack bam in the middle of his face.

"Call Levi," he whispered to Derek.

"What?" Derek's jaw dropped. "I was joking. I mean, he lives down the road and does have a chopper, but I mean, I don't-"

"Call in a favour," Eddie told him. "Do it now and do it quick."

Without any further explanation, Eddie ran toward the men from social services dragging Billy away, knocked them into the wall with a shoulder barge that had all the weight of his body behind it, and grabbed hold of the boy in his arms.

"Follow me," he told the mother, who obliged as he burst out the door and ran across the driveway.

Derek followed behind them, his phone at his ear. "Hi, Levi? You around this afternoon? ... Great, because I kind of have a favour to ask."

CHAPTER SEVENTEEN

*E*ddie struggled to keep his hold of Billy writhing in his arms. Not only was Billy's weight growing even more difficult to handle, his kicking out was making him difficult to keep hold of. The demon was furiously struggling, thrashing out his legs, swinging his hands, sticking his dirty nails into Eddie's face.

Eddie, reliant firmly on adrenaline, kept chanting prayers under his voice, hoping they would help to numb this demon's temper to a controllable level whilst they ran.

Derek and Jane, the boy's mother, kept pace with him, checking behind him as the two men from social services kept up.

"Where are we meeting him?" Eddie shouted at Derek, struggling to be heard above the wind.

"Football pitch, about half a mile away!"

"Half a mile?"

Eddie wasn't sure if he could manage half a mile. Not only was the demon flailing this boy's limbs out at him, his mother's crying was getting ridiculously distracting. She looked terrible, running beside him, attempting to keep up whilst begging for them to save her son. He could hear Derek's voice attempting to reassure her, but couldn't tell what he was saying. Eddie remained focussed on keeping his legs moving and holding the struggling Billy securely in his arms.

It was a stupid idea to have ever invited a sceptic along.

He understood what Derek was trying to do, and recognised that he had the best of intentions, but it had backfired terribly.

The sound of a helicopter batting its rotor blades appeared in the distance and it descended behind a group of trees.

That was fast.

Levi was a good man; he knew what was at stake. He owed him a debt of gratitude for this.

Approaching the field, he saw a thorny bush separating the escape from him.

The men approached. They reached out for Billy, even managed to grab hold of a hand.

Derek reached his foot out and tripped the man who was almost in reach, sending him flying onto his belly. The other guy was slightly more overweight, luckily for them, but was gaining quickly, almost within touching distance.

Eddie moved Billy into a firm fireman's lift, secured his grip, and leapt over the fence. Billy almost fell out of his arms, but Eddie dug his fingers into the boy's back, ignoring the yelps of pain amongst the shouts of abuse.

"You fucking cunt, you will die for this, you bastard!"

One minute he was calling me their saviour, the next he's calling me a cunt.

"Take off!" Eddie screamed at Levi, who was visible in the cockpit.

The rotor blade furiously rotated, rising the helicopter off the ground, hovering over the grass. Wind and leaves hit Eddie in the face, the aerodynamic resistance pushing him back. Despite the wind and his aching muscles, he managed to dive into the helicopter and throw Billy's body onto the floor, pinning him down with all his weight.

Looking up, he saw the mother jump on too. Derek grabbed hold of the landing skids and, as they rose into the air, wrestled himself onto the helicopter, allowing himself the satisfaction of watching the two men from social services come to a halt.

Eddie felt smug, but it didn't last long. The boy was still thrashing out at him, and the helicopter had no doors stopping the boy from throwing himself out of the helicopter.

Derek strapped the mother into the helicopter seatbelt and turned to Eddie. They shared eye contact for a moment, the urgency of the situation silently confirmed.

"Where we going?" Levi shouted over his shoulder, straight to business.

"Social services!" Derek screamed back and turned his head to Eddie. "Let's go, Eddie."

"How?" Eddie shrieked.

"Look, we have five minutes before we have the police find us, if that. A helicopter is hardly inconspicuous, we aren't going to be able to sustain this for long. We have to give him up."

Eddie nodded. Derek spoke sense.

"How long have I got?" he requested.

"Levi," Derek aimed at the pilot. "What's our ETA?"

"Seven minutes."

"You have seven minutes, Eddie."

Seven minutes?

He had never done an exorcism in seven minutes before. This wasn't a challenge, this was impossible.

"Derek, I can't do it. Even me, with this gift, I can't pray a demon out of a child's body in seven minutes."

The demon had ceased thrashing and just lay there cackling. It knew they had no chance; it knew it wasn't going anywhere. It had this child's body. It knew they couldn't do anything to remove it. It didn't need to thrash, it could just lay back and enjoy.

"You stand no chance…" the deep voice croaked.

Eddie bowed his head. All that effort getting to the helicopter, being chased down, for nothing. He could taste defeat; the bitter, old saliva of dehydration in his mouth.

The sound of the boy's mother whimpering faded behind the sound of the violent rotor blades keeping them in the air.

"You should lead us," the demon aimed at Eddie. "You are destined to lead us."

"Fuck — you!" he cried out. He was sick of demon's saying this stuff to him, constantly. He wished he could make it stop. That, mixed with despairing anger at failing this boy, made him feel sick.

"You can do it, Eddie," Derek said.

"No, I can't!"

"Not through prayer. Through other means."

Other means? What on earth was he on about?

"Eddie, you have been practising those spells, right?"

"Yes, but they all failed. I couldn't even do the chest thing to Jenny."

"Do it now."

"It won't work!"

"Then you won't lose anything."

Eddie bowed his head and closed his eyes. He couldn't stand letting people down. But it hadn't worked, and he'd tried it a fair few times.

"Four minutes," pointed out Levi.

Eddie looked to Derek. He looked so optimistic, looking at him expectantly, with such faith.

"You can do it," he whispered. Despite his voice getting lost in the sound of the helicopter, Eddie knew what he had said.

With a reluctant sigh, Eddie turned to the demon and put his hand on the boy's chest.

"De medio tollere, toll de medio. Manum tuam et peccator."

Nothing. As expected.

"Try it again!" Derek demanded.

"Three minutes," announced Levi.

He placed his hand on Billy's chest, ignoring the demon smirking at his failed attempts, feeling Derek watching over his shoulder.

"De medio tollere, toll de medio. Manum tuam et peccator."

The demon sniggered.

"You're saying it wrong." Derek placed his hand on Eddie's back.

"What?"

"You're saying 'man-oom' tuam. It's 'man-um' tuam."

Eddie's face dropped. Of course. How could he be so stupid?

He turned to the boy again, forcing his hand against the heart of this poor, possessed child, pressing with ferocity.

"One minute!"

Taking in a deep breath, Eddie prepared himself, then looked into the eyes of the demon.

"De medio tollere, tell de medio, manum taumtaum-" he said, correctly this time "- et peccator."

The demon screamed out in pain, the boy's chest rose into the air, mouth gasping, arms thrashing, fingers grasping.

Eddie saw a cloud of grey leave the boy's mouth, echoes of hooves and horns within the mix of smoke.

Then nothing.

The boy lay down. Still. His eyes opened slowly, focussing on Eddie, then on Derek, then on Jane.

"Mum?" he spoke. "Mum, is that you?"

Jane peeled off her seatbelt and threw herself toward her

son, grabbing him into a hug, holding him tight, furiously crying, telling him how much she loved him.

And, as the helicopter began its descent, ready to give the boy up and hope to avoid any reprimand from the law, Eddie looked at Derek.

Derek smiled proudly and gave Eddie a gentle nod. He had done it. He couldn't believe it.

CHAPTER EIGHTEEN

The heat in Kelly's room was intense. Palpable. She could feel nothing but lust.

Doug was on top and she was clawing her fingers into his back, tightly grabbing his skin. Sinking her fingers in, grabbing onto him, begging him not to stop.

She looked into his eyes.

A face appeared behind him.

She closed her eyes and ignored it.

She knew it was a dream. It was one of those weird situations where you know it's a dream, but you don't care. As it was just too damn good.

Suddenly, she was falling. Her bed opened up like a trap door and she was plummeting downwards. When she landed, she was lying on a wooden box, wearing nothing.

She was surrounded by pitch-black, perched upon a wooden crate, the only dimly lit object in the room.

Footsteps approached, with what sounded like metal, a chink that reminded her of cowboy films her dad used to watch when she was young.

"Who's there?" she shouted into the darkness, wishing that

she could wake up. "I know this isn't real, you don't frighten me."

"Even in your dreams..." came a hissing voice, "you can't escape us..."

She felt herself drop again.

Her eyes sprung open.

Her head lifted groggily and she forced her eyes wider, making sure she was now awake. She did not want to fall back asleep, as she knew she would likely return to her nightmare.

Leaning her head back, she noticed her pillow was gone. That's when she realised there was nothing supporting her back. In fact, there was nothing beneath her at all.

She turned her head as slowly as she could, dreading what she was going to find. She saw the wall to her side; that was still there at least. But her bed was below her. Far below her.

She pinched herself. It hurt.

She turned her head around more vigorously, and yelped. She was floating, mid-air, around five feet above her bed.

How am I doing this...

She panicked. Her heart pumped faster. She felt a breeze against her skin and smelt the early morning air as she noticed the window was open from the top, and she was right beside it.

She threw her hands out frantically, clambering, hoping to grab onto something. She reached her hand out to the wall, but as she did she moved slightly away from it. She was moving. Not only was she levitating, she was now being moved away from anything that could support her.

Tears ran down her cheeks and her arms lashed out again, with more ferocity, frantic attempts to grab onto something, or feel for something that would help support her.

"Let me down!" she cried out, her voice shaking.

Her whole body was kicking and thrashing, furiously attempting to do something to bring her back down to her bed.

Was this even real? Sure as she could feel the breeze from

the window against her face, she was floating. She believed it. But she had believed so many things, like voices, images, people, and none of them had been real.

Or so she had been taught.

"Let me down!" This time she screamed it, fighting through the tears in an attempt to find a commanding tone of voice, demanding whatever was toying with her to let her go.

With a sudden rush, she was thrown back down to her bed, landing with a thump that went into her back and caused a stabbing pain.

She wriggled and she writhed, moaning and crying. For what, she didn't even know anymore. It could have been the pain shooting through her back. It could have been the fact she was just levitating, or it could have just been the simple truth that she really didn't know what was real anymore.

Either way, she did not stop crying until her alarm clock went hours later. Even then she relied on her shower to wash her tears away.

* * *

KELLY PICKED up a sandwich and shuffled her way through the corridors of the university. She had barely managed to stay awake through her morning lectures and, if she was honest, she probably couldn't recollect a single thing that had been said.

As she was walking to find somewhere to have her lunch, a sign caught her eye. It indicated the direction to the Parapsychology and Paranormal Science Department.

Paranormal Science? What kind of subject was that? Were they actually investigating the paranormal?

Maybe they could help…

She entered the department, looking around, not entirely sure what she would expect. After all, aren't people who studied parapsychology normally nut jobs?

She entered a bare lecture theatre, finding an office at the end of it. She gently knocked and nudged the door open.

"Hello?"

A man with an open waistcoat, an open top button and a puzzled look on his face looked back at her. He rested his chin on his hand, softly stroking his goatee.

"Can I help you?" he requested, with a weary voice and tired eyes.

A few men in suits barged past her and into the office with boxes and collected a number of files, charging past her again as they removed them.

"Is this a bad time?" Kelly asked.

"It's not a great time; as you can see the university are putting us under investigation thanks to-" He halted, realising this was information she didn't need to know, and composed himself. "Sorry, miss, how can I help you?"

"Erm, I don't know really. If this is a bad time…"

"It's fine, best time as ever. My name is Derek, let's start there."

"Mine's Kelly."

"Nice to meet you, Kelly. Why don't you come in, take a seat, and tell me what's on your mind?"

Kelly entered the office and sat opposite Derek on the edge of her chair. She hesitated, not sure where to start.

"I… I've been having a few, like, disturbances."

"Disturbances?" Derek mused, sticking out his bottom lip. "And you consider these disturbances to be of paranormal origin."

"I… I don't know. I was sectioned before, and I thought it was over, but…"

"If you were diagnosed with mental health issues and treated for them, I think that probably gives you your explanation I'm afraid, Kelly."

"I woke up last night and I was levitating five feet in the air above my bed."

Derek fell silent. She had just blurted it out, hoping that this would be the person who did not believe she was crazy. Surely, out of everyone she had ever been honest with, this man would be the one to not have her sectioned. Following a moment of silence, she filled with self-doubt and regretted telling him.

"I'm sorry, I shouldn't have told you that, please forget I did."

She went to get up, but Derek waved her back down.

"It's okay, I'm not going to run off and tell people. You've come to the right person. Why don't you explain to me what exactly happened?"

"I don't know… that's the thing. I just woke up and I was mid-air and I couldn't get down. I went to touch the wall but whatever was doing it moved me away. I – I don't even know if it was real."

"Did it feel real? I mean, in your gut, real?"

No one had ever asked her that before. Anytime she was honest about these things, people's expression would immediately turn sombre and they would recoil in awkwardness, not sure what to say. This man didn't. He seemed intrigued, almost fascinated. This only made her more curious.

"I guess so."

"Kelly, this isn't something that people understand, or often even believe in. You see, people will hear you say this and assume you are crazy. I don't."

Kelly smiled. At last, someone who may accept her as something other than insane.

"Listen," he told her. "Ninety percent of the time it is mental health issues, but if you want to be sure…"

"I do, I really do."

"Then we can perform some tests, see what we find."

She grinned. She wasn't entirely sure why she was so elated, but she was; finally, somebody who could give her a different kind of help.

"Come back tomorrow at nine and we'll get started."

"Thank you," she said, standing up and shaking his hand, almost giddy. "Thank you so much."

He returned her smile and she practically danced out of the room.

That was, until it dawned on her that the idea of being haunted by the paranormal was far scarier than any mental health diagnosis.

CHAPTER NINETEEN

*K*elly shot out of bed, brushing her hair and teeth as quickly as she could. In fact, she arrived at the university so early that she had to force herself to wait, worried she may appear overly eager. Then she wondered why she was trying not to seem overly eager; it wasn't a date, it was a few tests. Surely there was no reason to seem overly eager about a few tests?

As 8:50 a.m. came around, she decided it was close enough that she could arrive without it being weirdly early. She drank the rest of the coffee she had been slowly sipping to pass the time, and made her way to the Parapsychology and Paranormal Science Department.

She poked her head around the corner of the lecture theatre to find Derek and another man setting up a contraption that looked like the beds she used to be restrained to in the mental health unit.

"Sorry I'm early…" she said weakly as she tiptoed in.

"Ah, Kelly." Derek greeted her with a welcoming smile. "We're not quite ready yet, but feel free to have a seat."

She meandered slowly to the front row of the lecture

theatre, decided the front row was overly keen, and made her way to the third row, staring with fascination at what they were doing.

They had a large area at the front of the lecture theatre to set up in. They had a bed — well, it was like a bed, except it looked more like a propped-up plank. Next to that was a machine, a camera with a tripod at the foot of the 'bed,' and a number of lights in a circle around it.

"What is all this?" she asked, but too quietly for either of them to hear, so she decided not to ask again. They were completely immersed in what they were doing, and it looked like anything else was tuned out. It seemed far more professional than what Kelly was expecting, though she wasn't quite sure what she was expecting. Either way, the manner in which they set up the equipment was like clockwork, efficiently collaborating to get everything ready. They had clearly done this before.

As soon as 9:00 a.m. arrived, they were ready. Derek turned to Kelly with a smile.

"I know this may seem intimidating from looking at it, but trust us, we know what we are doing. If you would come down here please."

Kelly nodded and walked toward them. Her knees felt suddenly weak. Her stomach twisted. She felt butterflies. She tried her best to calm herself.

"This is my partner in the paranormal, Edward King."

The other man offered his hand and Kelly shook it.

"Call me Eddie," he told her.

"Have a seat," Derek instructed, and Kelly complied, sitting on the edge of the make shift bed.

"What is all this stuff?"

"Good question. Please allow me to explain." He rushed to the camera at the end of the bed as Eddie continued to set up and program the equipment. "This is a camera triggered to flash and take a picture when something interferes with its ultraviolet light, or is of a certain frequency, as malevolent spirits often are."

He made his way to the machine Eddie was setting up. "This is a heart monitor. If you have ever been to a hospital, I am sure you will have seen one. This is as a matter of safety. We want to make sure your vitals are okay throughout, and if there is ever an irregularity, we will cease the experiment immediately. Speaking of which, place these on yourself please."

He handed some pads to Kelly. Funnily enough, she didn't need him to explain what they were; she'd had her vitals monitored many a time. She attached them to her forehead, over her heart, and to her wrist, as Derek darted to the lights.

"These are our lights, We won't be using the house lights today. Each of these are a different colour, allowing us to see any interference picked up by a different wavelength — gamma, what have you — it is all very complicated, but basically put, these lights pick up various things that indicate to us whether something is present that is of the paranormal. Satisfied?"

Taken aback by his request for her approval, she nodded vaguely.

"Right, if you will, Kelly, lay down and put your wrists and ankles through the restraints. Know that these are just for our safety should you lash out at any time — they will not be tightened, and if you wish to remove yourself from them at any point, you simply slide out of them."

As she laid down and placed her wrists and ankles in the restraints, she took them out and put them back in a few times. She felt a lot better knowing that she wasn't being fastened to the table, that she could still have free movement if she wished.

"Now, Kelly, listen to me, as this is important." He looked her dead in the eyes. "If, at any point, you wish to stop, or don't feel safe, or feel that this is getting too much for you, you say the word and we stop. But know that the more we prod you and the more we try, the more we will be able to be certain as to whether or not this problem you are having is of the demonic persuasion. Understood?"

Again, she nodded loosely. She realised her jaw was open and she closed her mouth. She let her head drift back and stared at the ceiling above her. It was very high up and had a plain pattern over cream coloured ceiling tiles.

"Eddie, I will let you stand back and see what you will, and I will measure the data. Okay?"

Eddie nodded. He backed up a few paces, closed his eyes and bowed his head.

Derek looked at him to check he was ready and took his concentration as indication to start. He backed up to the door, locked it, and turned off the lights.

Above her and to the left, Kelly could see the multiple lights they had set up shining over her. One was red, the other green, orange, blue, then red again. Directly behind her head was a white strip light.

"Kelly, are you ready?" Derek requested. She nodded.

"Eddie, we may begin," he whispered, taking a few steps back.

Kelly lifted her head, only able to see the top of Eddie from where he stood. She saw him keep his head down and lift his hands. He spread his palms out and moved them in slow, circular motions.

She dropped her head down for a few moments to rest her neck, which was hurting as she strained to see him.

When she looked up again, he was still moving his hand in a circular motion, but he had gotten faster, and he was going faster and faster still.

Kelly felt herself jolt. Her head flew back as if pulled back by an abrupt bolt of electricity.

The camera at the end of the bed flashed.

The heart rate monitor bleeped quicker.

Her fists clenched, her legs tightened, and she wasn't sure why.

The camera flashed again. And again.

She scrunched her face as she felt something move, a throbbing pain travelling from her toes and up her body until it reached her head.

Her mouth dropped.

Her head wilted to the side as she spewed vomit all over the floor.

The camera flashed. And again. And again. And again.

The red light flickered.

The beep on the heart rate monitor sped up. *Be-beep, be-beep, be-beep, be-beep*.

Camera flashed.

Red light flickered.

Beep beep beep beep beep beep beep beep.

She screamed out, but it wasn't her voice coming from her. It was someone else's.

She slipped away, like she wasn't really there, like it was her body but she was just a passenger watching it take a ride.

The red light flickered quickly, so fast it almost blinded her, and the orange light joined in. The camera flashed like it was in a race with the heart-rate monitor.

She screamed once more, then it all went blank.

A peaceful moment of darkness ensued.

When she opened her eyes, she was in the foetal position upon the floor.

"Kelly, are you okay? Can you hear me?"

She looked up and Derek was knelt over her. The guy who had introduced himself as Eddie was sat in the corner of the room, dabbing blood from his face, breathing heavily.

She looked over her shoulder at the rest of the room. The bed was overturned, smoke was rising from the camera, and the lights lay on top of each other, smashed. The restraints were still around her wrists and her ankles, but they were ripped, as if they had been removed by force.

She peered up at Derek, who had his hand on her shoulder. He offered her a towel. She took it and dabbed her forehead. She hadn't realised how drenched in sweat she was, but when she looked down she saw her clothes sticking to her.

"What happened?" she asked, finding that her throat was sore.

"Kelly, I think we need to have a conversation," Derek told her.

* * *

KELLY SAT in the office with a towel around her and a hot chocolate in her hands, kindly delivered to her by Eddie. Derek was sat beside her and Eddie was sat opposite her, both gawking at her, like they were in some kind of perplexed daze.

"Guys, you're both staring at me…"

"We do apologise," Derek insisted. "It's just, once you hear what we have to say, you may understand why."

"You're starting to freak me out a bit."

"Well, Kelly, you are going to need to prepare yourself for what you're about to hear."

She sipped on her hot chocolate and shifted her gaze between them.

"What's going on?"

Derek sighed and looked around, as if he was trying to pluck a clear and concise explanation from thin air. He went to say something, but couldn't, and in his despondence turned to Eddie, who bowed his head and looked at Kelly.

"Kelly, I have a gift," he told her. "I am able to manipulate the paranormal, to command demons. I am able to pick up on when someone else is dealing with a presence, an entity… that is not of the natural world. And I was able to pick up on something quite strongly in you."

"So I'm not insane? Something is haunting me?"

Eddie lifted his head back with an awkward sigh. He looked torn, unable to answer, so she looked to Derek, who too was darting his eyes around the room just as uncomfortably.

"Guys, please, just tell me."

"When we do these tests, you see," Derek took over, "we expect minimal results as an indication. If the camera flickers say, once or twice, we assume there is something there. If the other lights show something moving before it, or if Eddie can see something that he provokes out of you, we take that as an indication and pursue with further tests that may lead us to an exorcism."

"So you saw these things with me?"

"My dear, the camera didn't just flash once or twice as we occasionally see. It flickered continuously for the duration until it burnt out. The lights that normally pick up some unusual movement in the air, they smashed and rose from the ground. Eddie himself was taken over and overpowered by something that sent him across the room and beat him to a pulp, and he has never been unable to command a demon so long as I've known him."

Kelly stared at Derek, not quite knowing what to make of it all. This was clearly a bad omen. Either that, or these were two nuts taking part in her delusion. Whatever their reasons, at least this was an explanation that made sense to her, however bizarre it seemed.

"So you think I'm being haunted?"

"Kelly, you are more than being haunted," Eddie told her assertively. "You are being possessed. By something far more powerful than our everyday demon."

"Like what?"

"I don't know, I'm afraid. Maybe a king of demons, a commander of hell – Jesus, it may even be the devil himself."

That's when Derek became alert. He looked wide-eyed to Eddie. The prophecy. He remembered what it had said.

Come the new millennium, the world will hail the arrival of the first coming of hell. The son of the devil. He will embrace the world and his powers will control all demons that stand in his way.

In this time, the devil will rise, taking the body of a human. Fate will align the son of the devil with its God and it will give way to his true fate.

"WHAT THE HELL is going on in here?" came an angry, authoritarian voice.

Derek opened his office door and bestowed his eyes upon the livid dean of the university.

"We were just doing some tests, it will be cleaned up soon. I will replace it."

"You certainly will not," he replied. That was when Derek noticed a few other members of the university board, along with security and Jason Aslan.

"What is going on?" demanded Derek.

"We have been given footage of you and Edward King tormenting a young boy."

Eddie and Derek emerged from the office, sharing inquisitive looks.

"My files have already been taken away by the police, thanks to this man." Derek gestured toward Jason Aslan, who stood with his arms folded. "What more is there to say?"

"I am afraid, Professor," the dean spat, pronouncing each

venomous syllable through gritted teeth, "that the university will be suspending both you and Edward, pending our own investigation. I would appreciate it if you could remove your-self from the university's property so we can carry out the enquiry without interference."

Derek looked over his shoulder at Eddie, and they exchanged looks of concern. Before they could stop them, security had found Kelly and taken her away for medical help, leaving Eddie and Derek to have to explain why a young, female student was in their office with injuries and a shocked expression on her face.

They found themselves leaving the university without objection.

CHAPTER TWENTY

Kelly wasn't sure what to make of everything as she walked home. She wasn't entirely sure what had happened to her, but every part of her ached, from the muscles in her legs to the thumping in her head. It was a night off for her and Doug tonight, but she considered calling him, feeling like she really needed him.

She paused at the pedestrian crossing but no cars decided to stop for her. She went to go a few times, but cars kept turning the corner and zooming past her.

"Dick!" she shouted at one of them as they sped into the distance, the loud rev of the sports car engine lingering long after they had gone.

Enough was enough. She stepped onto the crossing, so fed up she didn't care if someone chose to run her down.

She made her way through the courtyard of the halls of residence and fumbled in her bag for her keys. She grew even more agitated as she struggled to find them. Then, once she had found them, every attempt to grab them just fumbled them further away.

Sighing, she leant her forehead against the door. When your

keys are running away from you, you know it's time to take a nap. She was growing tired of pure bad luck.

Finally, she grabbed hold of her keys and withdrew them. They were attached to her headphones and she had to yank them away a few times to get them free. She slid the key into the door and opened it, making her way up the stairs.

Possessed by a demon? That's what they had told her, right? And not just any demon, but a powerful king or commander in hell. It just seemed so farfetched — but they had their own department in the university, so someone must have had enough faith in them to fund them.

Although, they did seem to be in a spot of bother as she left. The university were clearly unhappy with what they had been doing with people they were supposedly helping. Maybe they were into something sinister, and they were trying to convince her that she was possessed so they could be even more invasive with her. Maybe it was a pure exploitation ploy.

Or maybe they were the ones who were nuts.

The simple explanation is that I have mental health issues, she told herself. And it was true. She had always believed in the simplest answer being the likeliest. She had learnt about the theory in one of her lectures about the psychology of logic — it was called Occam's razor. The theory that a scientist must accept the simplest answer as most often correct.

But there was something about what they said that made sense. A niggling thought at the back of her head, and it wouldn't go away.

She made her way along her corridor to her room and could hear noises coming from Mindy's room next to hers. She strained herself to try to listen to what it was.

"Uh! Uh! Yeah, come on!"

Oh my God she's having sex!

She glanced at her watch. It was 11:00 a.m. Yes, she would

normally be in lectures right now, that she had missed for these tests, but still — it was oddly early to be having sex.

She shrugged her shoulders and put the key in the lock to her room. *To each their own, I guess.*

"Uh! Oh! God yeah!"

As she turned the key in her door Mindy grew even louder, getting seemingly closer to her climax. Kelly took this as a good sign, in the hope that she was nearly finished.

"Oh my God you are so good! No wonder she likes you!"

Kelly held her door open mid-air. What did she just say?

"Uh! Oh God, yes, Doug, Doug!"

She froze. A shot of adrenaline raced through her. Her arms shook, a sickening feeling mounting in her gut and rising up to her throat.

"Oh, Doug, yes!"

"Mindy!" Kelly screeched at the top of her voice. She was a little taken aback, as she had never known herself to sound so aggressive. She positioned herself in front of Mindy's door and clenched her fists beside her waist. Her leg was bouncing with angry anticipation, her head shaking.

She felt suddenly ready for a fight — a feeling she had never felt before.

"Kel?" came a startled reply from inside the room.

"Open the door."

"Can you come back later, babe?"

The door before her shook. Just small vibrations, as if it was wobbling back and forth in a slight earthquake, just rattling. But there wasn't an earthquake. And Kelly wasn't entirely sure why the door was shaking, but it was.

"Open the fucking door!"

Without having any time to reply, Mindy's door soared off its hinges and sailed rabidly through the air, smashing through the far window of Mindy's room.

Kelly crossed the threshold. She hadn't walked in, in fact

she wasn't sure how she entered, but she somehow found herself inside.

Mindy poked her head up from under the covers.

"Kelly?"

Kelly swiped her right hand through the air and the duvet swept away, revealing Mindy and Doug's sweaty, naked bodies pressed up against each other.

Mindy and Doug appeared petrified. Kelly wasn't fully aware that was because her hands were smoking. She didn't realise she had risen two feet off the floor and she hadn't a clue it was because her eyes had turned dark red.

"Kelly, please stop!"

Kelly's lungs burnt as her voice screamed, except it wasn't her voice filling the room, but a whole load of voices, from deep wails to high shrieks, all at the same time.

Items glided off the shelf. A group of text books bashed against the opposite wall. One of the shelves snapped in half. The bed rattled to the point Doug and Mindy had to clutch onto the side for dear life.

Doug attempted to scarper; he jumped to his feet and went to rush past Kelly, but he did not get far. As soon as he reached Kelly's side, her hands were around his throat and she was holding him mid-air, his feet dangling.

"Ke… ly…" he sputtered, choking helplessly, struggling for breath.

"Kelly, stop!" begged Mindy, but the wind spinning around the room, taking objects in its wake, silenced her voice.

Doug punched Kelly's arm, which loosened her grasp for a moment and he dropped to the floor, clutching his throat. It was sore, and he felt every bit of the pain as he traced the red line she had left.

Kelly elevated her arms and Doug instantly rose, spiralling across the air and flattening against the wall above the bed.

Mindy had her mobile phone out, with 9-9-9 dialled in.

Kelly noticed and the phone malfunctioned, spitting an electric shock at Mindy's cheek, who dropped the phone out of her hand.

Kelly kept one hand in the air, projecting Doug into place with a snarl upon her face. Mindy tried looking into her eyes, tried to see the person that Kelly was, but that person had left. She did not see Kelly any more. This was something else, something hell-bent on using her fury for its own means.

Kelly lifted her spare arm and slashed it downwards, producing three deep claw marks against Doug's chest. Blood splattered against the wall, the bed sheets, and Mindy's face, who covered her face and rubbed her eyes in an attempt to get the blood off her.

Doug squealed in agony, grasping at his gaping wounds, each touch only making the pain that bit more excruciating.

Mindy got to her knees and crawled toward her. Kelly threw Doug across the room and slammed him into a wall, forcing him to fall onto the floor via his face, where he lay, dipping in and out of consciousness. This left Kelly free to deal with Mindy.

She raised her hand and Mindy's naked, flailing body rose, hanging mid-air, directly in front of Kelly.

"Please…" she begged. "Stop…"

Kelly tilted her head slightly, looking at Mindy peculiarly.

"If you like being fucked so much," came the words out of Kelly's mouth, through numerous deep, booming voices, very different to a young, teenage woman, "then so be it."

Kelly held her hand out in a claw, pointing upwards. Her nails grew, with a brown, stale tint stained over the protruding claws.

Whilst staring at Mindy, she lunged her hand upwards and tightened her nails into place.

Mindy screamed in agony without stopping for a breath, grabbing onto her crotch, weeping through begs and screams.

She writhed in pain, blood not just trickling, but pouring down her inner thighs. Kelly lifted her hand up even further and Mindy howled in anguish.

Kelly's feet landed on the ground. She put her hands by her side and Mindy dropped to the floor, where she rolled around, whimpering desperately.

Almost as soon as her feet touched the ground, police burst in through the door behind Kelly and shoved her against the wall, restraining her hands behind her back. From the moment they handcuffed her, walked her to the car and took her to jail, she did not stop smiling.

CHAPTER TWENTY-ONE

"*S*o you mean, it actually worked?" Jenny's eyes lit up, her jaw dropped and her smile grew. She was elated, hugely impressed at the feat of Eddie's power.

Eddie gushed, delighted to have prompted such a reaction. It made a nice break from the animosity he and Derek were facing at the university.

"Yeah, I was just not saying one of the words right," he recalled to her. "Once I had corrected it, it sucked the demon right out of its mouth and it disappeared into grey smoke."

Jenny nudged Lacy next to her, who was also impressed, though not nearly as much as Jenny. Lacy was Jenny's more relaxed, laid-back girlfriend, whom Eddie adored. He had been there when they first got together and witnessed how much controversy they'd had to overcome, mainly from Jenny's conservative parents. It was warming to see them sitting here a decade later, strong as ever.

"So what are we trying now?" Jenny enquired, crossing her legs and sitting forward on the garden bench as Lacy rubbed her back and watched on with intrigue.

"Well," began Eddie, lifting his book up and glancing

over the spell before him. "This is a much higher level kind of spell. It's far beyond pumping a demon out of a boy's chest."

"What is it?"

"Conjuring a fireball."

Jenny raised her eyebrows, stumped, turning to Lacy and acknowledging her impressed reaction too.

"Well, fuck," Lacy said, noticing Jenny was too jaw-dropped to reply. "Why not, eh?"

Eddie nodded and turned toward the tree across the garden.

"You did say you wanted to get rid of this tree, right?"

"Yes," Lacy nodded. "And we didn't want to pay for a tree surgeon. This is a good solution."

Eddie nodded, dropping the book to the floor beneath him, looking over the spell. He put one foot in front of the other, preparing his stance, focussing his eyes ahead.

"So what do you have to do?" Jenny enquired.

"It says I have rotate my arms around each other, say the incantation, then throw my arms forward. It should just, like, fire out of me."

"And there's no chance of us getting hit, right? I mean, I love you, but I don't want to burn to death."

"I think you're fine. Who knows if it will even work?"

"That's what you said before."

Eddie nodded. True, he had said that. Nevertheless, he still worried, still hesitant, honestly not expecting it to succeed.

He readied himself, closed his eyes, took in a big deep breath — then focussed ahead.

He rotated his hands around in a 360-degree angle, spinning them in a circle, slowly at first, then faster and faster. As his arms sped up, he glanced at the book to remind himself of the words, then looked dead ahead.

"Igne egredientur, igne egredientur," he spoke, ensuring he

was saying it right this time, enunciating every sound. "Igne egredientur, igne egredientur."

His hands flickered. A spark ignited quickly and went out. It gave him a glimmer of hope.

"Igne egredientur, igne egredientur."

His hands moved quicker and quicker, more and more sparks igniting. He felt energy flowing through his arms, blood quickening pace, his fingertips singing with heat.

"Igne egredientur, igne egredientur."

His heart skipped a beat, his gut lurched forward, and he grew hopeful. He was vaguely aware of Jenny and Lacy from the corner of his eyes, avidly watching, but was too focussed to direct his attention elsewhere.

"Et ignis furorem." His voice rose, more and more flames alighting and disappearing.

His eyes opened wide and he screamed the final part of the spell.

"Converte ad lucem vitae!"

He threw his arms forward, his muscles rattling and his bones shaking with such ferocity he thought they were going to fly right out of their sockets.

And from his hands before him flew...

Nothing.

The tree remained. The flickers had ceased. No flames exuded from his pores.

He had failed.

He fell to his knees, the energy the spell had zapped from him taking his legs from beneath him. He dropped onto his back.

Next thing he knew, Jenny was over him, screaming for Lacy.

"Lacy, we need you!"

She shoved Jenny out of the way and took over, her nursing skills coming into action.

"What…" Eddie tried, but found his voice straining.

"His nose is bleeding!" Jenny cried out.

"He'll be fine," Lacy told her. "He's just suffering a bit of concussion. Let's get him to the sofa."

He may have been dizzy and unaware, but he knew enough to know the spell had failed. His scattered thoughts flew that reminder around his head again and again.

He awoke around an hour later and took a few paracetamols, feeling fine. Though, not fine enough to attempt the spell again.

CHAPTER TWENTY-TWO

*I*t took a dozen police officers to drag Kelly into a cell. Sergeant Jack Sony was the mental health liaison officer and was called as soon as they checked her background and saw that she had previously been sectioned.

Once he arrived, he stood with the custody sergeant and watched her through the cell window.

She was in a manic frenzy, bashing from side to side of the cell, screaming obscenities and blasphemous threats, causing more damage to herself than the walls around her.

"We can't leave her like this," Jack told his colleague, folding his arms.

"What do you suggest, we restrain her?"

"No, she's not mentally fit to stay here. We need to have her sectioned. Call the doctor and ask them to send someone."

"Okay."

He turned to leave and Jack put his hand on his shoulder to stop him.

"Actually, best ask him to send a team. Then get the papers needed from the Crown Prosecution Service to delay her charges pending assessment of her mental stability."

Jack remained outside the cell, peering in on her. She had been attacking the walls for six hours, she must have been bruised to hell. And still, she showed no sign of letting up.

* * *

JASON SAT with Ava on his lap, listening to her reading a book about Tim and Tom and their journey to go to the sweetshop or something, following the words along with his eyes, his mind somewhat absent.

Once she was finished, he gave her a hug, congratulated her, and told her there were some chocolate mice in the fridge as a treat. She sped off to retrieve them.

Jason sat up and watched Linda across the room with Mia on her lap, both asleep. He couldn't help but smile. What a lovely sight; all those nights back when they first got married she would fall asleep in that chair, then once they had Harper, she would fall asleep with Harper on her lap in that chair, and now, here she was, with Mia, doing the same.

History sure does have a way of repeating itself.

The doorbell rang and Jason stood, pausing for a second as he willed the stiffness from his legs. This was the problem with getting older; everything you don't want getting stiff damn well does.

"Must be Harper," he said, despite knowing his wife was fast asleep and wouldn't be able to hear him.

He straightened his back and, ignoring the old-man pain he felt, he hobbled his way to the front door and opened it.

There, on his porch, stood Derek. Drenched from the pouring down rain, his clothes soaked through and his hair flattened to his head.

"What the hell are you doing here?" Jason growled.

"Mr Aslan, please, if I could just have a minute of your time."

"Damn it, my grandchildren are here. What is wrong with you? Have you no dignity?"

"Please, I just need a minute of your time."

"I have nothing to say to you!" Jason snapped and went to close his door.

"Well, I have something to say to you," Derek replied forcefully, holding out his hand and halting the door. "I'm not here to start an argument. One minute of your time and then I will never bother you again, you have my word."

Jason hesitated, looking the man up and down. He was wet, he was desperate; he almost pitied him that his belief in the irrational had driven him to this. Still, a promise of never being bothered by him again was tempting. He looked pathetic.

"Come through to the study," he barked. "I'll get you a damn towel."

"Thank you, thank you so much."

Derek shuffled his feet on the mat to dry them and was ushered into a study, Jason closing the door before anyone else saw him. After a few seconds, Jason joined him and shoved a towel his way.

"Thank you," he acknowledged, and half-heartedly dried his hair. "Can we sit?"

"Sure."

They both sat on the easy chairs and looked at one another. Derek dried his hair for a few more moments, then laid the towel down on his lap, hesitating, contemplating what to say next.

"This is where you tell me what you want," Jason prompted.

"Right, yes, okay," Derek stumbled. "I do not blame you for what you have done, you must know that. Were I in your position, and I witnessed such a thing with the belief system you hold, I would be inclined to do the same."

"Right," Jason accepted, then shrugged his shoulders as if to say, 'so what?'

"But what we have now is a girl in a huge amount of trouble. She has the highest signs of possession we have ever seen. We have been disallowed from carrying out our activities, but that is not going to stop us, Mr Aslan. We are determined to help this girl, whatever the consequences."

"That's fine. What's it got to do with me?"

"She has been sectioned, Mr Aslan. She was arrested for an attack and was moved to a psychiatric unit shortly after. It is crucial — no, it is imperative, that we get to this girl before it is too late."

"Like I said, what's it got to do with me?"

Derek sighed, bowed his head and closed his eyes.

"We can't get to her, Jason. Thanks to what has happened, we can't even go near her as a visitor, not on our own. We need your credentials. We need you to get us in."

Jason looked Derek up and down. Was this a joke? He saw Derek's face was deadly serious and he burst out laughing.

"Are you serious? Why the hell would I do that?"

"I don't know, good will? Doing the right thing?"

"Doing the right thing," he echoed, ceasing the laughing and turning serious. "Doing the right thing would be to ensure that you get locked up for the rest of your life, away from any member of society you can affect with your bullshit."

"I will make you a deal. On the condition you stand and watch, and you may film, but this time you do not interfere."

"What kind of deal do you think I would make?"

"The boy you saw showed signs of possession. This girl is the living embodiment of it. If there was ever going to be clear, unarguable proof that the paranormal exists, and it exists in demon form, it would be here. You would have your proof. And you would not be able to argue with it."

"You already offered me that."

"Yes, but this is the deal I am prepared to make. Should I not convince you, should you not take this as unequivocal evidence, I will remove myself from the post I hold. You won't need a court order, or an investigation, or a police charge – I will leave the university and not engage in any of this activity ever again."

Jason paused for thought. This was an opportunity. The university was investigating him, but chances are they would find nothing strong enough and he would be reinstated. If he filed a police charge, they would need to gather enough evidence to arrest him, then find enough to take to a judge; it could take months, maybe even years. Even then it may not pan out; the evidence could be poor, Derek's lawyer could be too good, the jury could be religious nut jobs themselves.

But this deal... that he would stop completely, and if Jason could prevent anyone else being harmed after the hundreds these frauds had already brought harm to, that would be the pinnacle of his career. That could be his defining achievement. That would truly make him one of the greats.

"You have a deal."

Derek smiled a smile so huge it almost spread across the entirety of his face. He stuck out a hand and Jason gratefully shook it.

What a fool.

CHAPTER TWENTY-THREE

*D*erek could see that Eddie looked a little nervous. He was avoiding eye contact and he kept pulling the expression he pulled when he was deep in thought. Derek had never seen him like this before. It was startling to see someone who could do the things Eddie could displaying such apprehension.

After Jason had shown his identification, they were led to a secure medical room and the security guard stood outside. As soon as they were inside, Derek took a plank of wood from his bag and slid it between the door handles. To make doubly sure, he also tied the handles together with rope.

Jason raised his eyebrows.

"If we get interrupted, it will ruin the whole thing and leave her in a far worse position than she is in now," Derek informed him.

The coldness of the room hit them; it was always cold in this situation, but it felt like the temperature was even lower. Derek could feel the moisture in the air against this face and goosepimples grew on his skin. He glanced at Jason, who avoided eye contact and set his camera up at the end of the bed, tightening his jacket around himself.

"You'd have thought they'd turn the heating up in here or something," Jason complained.

"You think it would make any difference if they did?" Derek asked, and Jason shot him a look you would give to a child who was intentionally being difficult.

Eddie approached the bed Kelly lay upon. The sound of her breathing filled the room; deep, croaky, and slow. Her eyes were open, revealing fully dilated pupils and red, bloodshot veins. She stared at the ceiling without blinking or moving her eyes whatsoever.

For the first time in this situation, Derek felt worried. Not only was Eddie clearly anxious, he was facing something that may potentially bring out the dark side in him. Derek began to wonder if he should let Eddie do this, and realised there wouldn't really be much he could do to stop him.

"Jason," Eddie said, softly and calmly. Derek recognised a bit of shakiness in his voice. "I must ask you to not speak directly to it, nor do you intervene with anything we do. It is crucial."

"Okay."

"I mean it. If you see nothing, we will stick to our word. But if you run off to grab security at the first sign of distress, you will ruin everything."

"I said I heard you."

Eddie turned his focus to the girl who lay in front of him. Her wrists and ankles were restrained to the metal table, though Eddie knew that if the thing inside her was as powerful as they thought, these restraints wouldn't hold her for long.

"Kelly, my name is Edward King. I am here to help you."

Kelly did not react.

Her gaze was fixed on the ceiling above her. Her breath lingered visibly in the air, grey, floating up to the ceiling.

"If you can hear me, Kelly, hang tight. We will get rid of

whatever is holding you captive. If you can, we need you to fight also. We will do all we can from the outside, but you need to fight from the inside."

Eddie glanced over his shoulder at Derek, fear spread across his face. Between them, they shared a moment of understanding, a moment when they both knew what they were up against.

Derek, because he had run the tests.

Eddie, because he had felt it.

He felt it in his bones, his blood, his mind. He was in the presence of something not only powerful, but full of unadulterated evil.

It filled his body with fury, and he was doing all he could to keep himself calm.

"I speak now to the entity within. I give you the opportunity to release God's child and return to Hell."

Kelly grinned.

"I give you this opportunity now, because I will not give you any mercy."

Kelly cackled. It was deliberate, with each "ha" sarcastically pronounced, her voice inexplicably deep.

"Demon, what is your name?"

Its cackles grew. Eddie became irritable. He continued calming himself, adamant that he would sustain his authority.

This thing was affecting him too much and he couldn't understand why.

"In the name of the Father, the Son and the Holy Ghost, I demand of you, demon, tell me your name."

"My name…" the demon muttered.

Several books flew off the shelf across the room and Eddie had to duck out the way to avoid being struck.

Jason turned his head to Derek, wide-eyed, unable to believe what he just saw.

"You think you can take on *me?*" the demon requested, twisting its face toward Eddie, grinning at the impudence.

"The Holy Church venerates you as her guardian and protector. Tell me your name."

"It is you..." the demon uttered, its eyes transfixed upon Eddie. "I have drawn you here, and you came..."

"I do not know you, demon. To the Lord, entrusted the souls of the redeemed to be led into Heaven, he demands you tell us your name."

"My son... you are my son..."

Eddie could not move. His son? Not only was he claiming, as every other demon claimed, to know him, he was claiming him as his son?

"I am not your son."

"My son... my heir..."

"I am not your heir!"

"Eddie," Derek snapped. "Focus!"

Eddie trembled, bowing his head, closing his eyes and drawing in breath.

"In the name of Jesus Christ our Saviour," he persisted, "tell me your name."

"You ask me my name," it spoke, multiple low-pitch voices produced all at once. "You ask me in *your* name and I will tell you."

"Fine. In my name, tell me, demon, what is yours?"

The room shook. Beakers and empty needles vibrated off the far tables and smashed upon the ground. The lights sparked, the bed Kelly's body lay upon battered against the floor.

Jason stood back, his mouth agape.

"My name is Lucifer."

The restraints snapped off its wrists and the bed shot out from beneath it, smashing into the wall. Kelly's body lingered in the air and rose above Eddie, its fists clenched, the whole room turning into pandemonium as objects soared furiously and lights seized on and off.

Derek and Jason were pushed off their feet in the commotion and they clung to the walls, trying not to get swept away in the ferocious wind battering chaotically around the room.

"No, it can't be!" Eddie fell to his knees. "You lie!"

"Eddie, focus!" Derek shouted, but his voice was lost and Eddie ignored it.

"You cannot be Lucifer."

"I am." Its voice filled the room, making their ear drums ache. "I am Lucifer, Satan, the devil himself."

The doors rattled with the sound of people trying to get in, reacting to the noise, trying to barge the door open without success.

The camera Jason clung to exploded and he flung his arms in front of himself to shield his eyes. The hurricane of the room took his feet out from beneath him, hurtling him from one wall to the other.

"And you, Jason Aslan," the demon boomed. "You think Linda is safe from me?"

"What?" Jason pushed himself to his knees and struggled to his feet. "What did you say?"

"You think Harper is safe from me?"

"Jason!" Eddie screamed. "Remember what I said, don't listen to it! It will say things to get to you, stand back!"

Jason didn't listen. He persisted toward the beast, his face filling with rage.

"You think Ava is safe from me? Mia?"

"You leave them out of this!"

"*I will rip them limb from limb.*"

Jason sprinted toward it. It just lifted its arm and Jason rose into the air. The demon straightened itself so it was floating vertically, looking in Jason's eyes, who squirmed helplessly in mid-air.

"You dare oppose me?"

"We drive you from us, unclean spirit!" Eddie screamed against the wind, endeavouring to save Jason by continuing the ritual. "All satanic powers, all infernal invaders, all wicked legions, assemblies and sects, we command you, leave this woman be!"

The demon didn't even react. No flinching, no quivering, nothing. It remained as powerful as it ever was, watching Jason cower before it.

"Eddie, we need to end this, it's no good!" Derek put his hand on his shoulder. "We need to go!"

"What about Jason?"

Eddie stepped forward.

The demon withdrew its hands, holding its fingers out in a claw, looking upon Jason like a king would a rat. Jason returned the gaze with eyes full of fear.

"God's word made flesh commands you! He who saved our race, outdone through your envy commands you. I command you! Release them!"

"Shut up," said the demon without even turning its head, and Eddie was sent flying onto his backside.

With one sadistic smile and a swipe of the arm, a line of blood drew across Jason's neck. He clambered for air, grabbing his throat, choking.

"No!" bellowed Eddie, but it was no good.

Jason suffocated in the air before the devil.

No matter how much Eddie tried, he couldn't get any closer.

The demon's claw sliced through one side of Jason's throat and out the other, splattering blood over the walls. Jason's head tore off and dangled from his neck by a piece of skin.

The demon screamed and the head flew clean off, bashing against the wall and falling to the floor next to its body.

It turned to Eddie, who was cowering, shaking, terrified.

"Leave this one," the demon commanded, nodding toward Derek. "Then come find me. We have much to do."

It ascended to the window at the top of the room. It shattered and the demon left.

The objects dropped, the wind ceased, and the room resumed its initial calmness.

Eddie and Derek were alone.

Derek did his best to drag Eddie away, but it was no good. He was inconsolable, his desolate eyes not faltering from the sight of Jason's head severed from its body.

"For false Christs and false prophets will arise, and will show great signs and wonders, so as to mislead, if possible, even the elect."

    (Matthew 24:24)

CHAPTER TWENTY-FOUR

*T*he cold hit Kelly like a bucket of ice. The morning sun was only slightly visible, poking through the clouds in the winter sky, and she could feel a strong chill in the air. She felt herself shiver as her senses regained themselves.

Huddling her arms around her chest, she felt nothing but skin. Her clothes were gone.

Her skin hair stood on end, frozen cold. Her naked body shivered as she lifted her head up to figure out where she was. Her vision was taking time to refocus. She reacted quickly to the feeling of itching over her skin and swiftly brushed a whole colony of ants off her body.

She knelt up, covering herself, humiliated at the thought of someone seeing her like this, until she realised she needn't worry; there wasn't another soul for as far as she could see. She was in some kind of woodland area, next to an open field, a fence in the distance.

She gagged. Her whole body convulsed and her nose blocked out all smells. A hot, lucid feeling ran up her throat and she spewed out a large amount of sick. Once she had gotten the first lot out, she felt the similar feeling rising up inside her again, and she brought up more sick; most of it red, bloody, and full of raw, undigested pieces of meat.

She stumbled to a tree and leant against it, coughing up the last of what was left in her gut. She whimpered helplessly, distressed that she couldn't understand where she was or why she was there, distraught that she was unclothed, and perturbed she couldn't help the feeling there was more vomit to come.

She went to take a few steps forward and stumbled over, her legs in agony, shooting pains going up and down her calf. She crawled a few steps forward and forced herself up, mentally urging herself to surge on through the pain.

She made it to an open field and her bones gave way, her muscles becoming void, her hands and knees landing in a squelch of mud.

"Hello?" she shouted out, vaguely optimistic that someone might hear her. "Hello?"

Her voice reverberated around the area without response. Looking back and forth at the frostbitten grass and crisp, icy leaves, she forced herself across the field toward the fence in the distance, wrapping her arms tightly around her chest in an attempt to both warm herself and cover her body.

Tears fell. Her gut felt terrible. She was freezing and mortified. In the middle of nowhere. Naked. Disgraced.

How was she going to get out of this?

The only thing she could do was cry. She felt pathetic in doing it, but she didn't know what else to do. She just wished this wasn't happening, that she was home, tucked up warmly in bed. In pyjamas.

How did I even get here?

She reached the fence. A foul stench hit her, forcing her to retch once more. It was a potent smell of rotting flesh and decaying meat filling the air like smoke from a fire. The further she willed herself forward, the stronger the repulsive odour became.

The sun was rising higher in the sky, indicating to her that morning had fully arrived. Her shivering grew more vigorous and she could focus on nothing but how cold she was and how obscene the smell in the air was.

She reached another fence and knelt on it, peering around at the adjoining field. That's when the cause of the smell revealed itself, sending her to her knees, vomiting the contents of her stomach once more.

An endless row of dead cows were laid out as far as she could see, next to a row of dead sheep. These animals weren't just dead; they were battered, slaughtered, mercilessly murdered. Their stomachs were exposed, gutted, disembowelled, sliced, and on many of them their heads were severed from their body.

Entrails were strewn and scattered across the fields until almost all the green was covered in red. Intestines, bowels, livers, hearts, all spread across, opened, broken into, torn apart into vile fragments, as if someone had ripped them open.

After being sick she fell to her knees and sobbed.

Did I do this?

Of course not, she wasn't capable.

How would she know? She hadn't any idea how she ended up where she was. The last thing she remembered was… hell, she didn't even know what the last thing she remembered was. Everything was hazy.

She was startled by the sound of a gasp and she turned around instantly. A man in a trench coat with a big moustache and flat cap stood behind her, clearly a farmer.

"Please help me…" she begged.

Without hesitation, the man took off his coat, placed it around her and guided her toward his tractor.

* * *

"THERE YOU ARE, DEAR," said the farmer's wife, who had introduced herself as Mildred, handing Kelly a hot chocolate. She was elderly and pleasant, someone who could make an adult feel like they were a six-year-old visiting Grandma's house once again.

Kelly was still shivering, but the roaring fire next to her was helping her get warm. She was wearing some of the farmer's old clothes. They were too big, but the thick, woolly jumper she had wrapped around her was helping her feel warm.

Mildred and her husband, who had introduced himself as Bill, sat opposite her, staring awkwardly.

"Would you like us to call the police for you?"asked Mildred, looking so concerned.

Kelly had a flash, a recent memory pushing itself to the forefront of her mind. She was in a cell. She was being restrained. Dozens of police grabbing hold of her, dragging her kicking and screaming.

No, the police were the last people she wanted.

"No, thank you," she said, barely audibly, and took a sip of her drink.

"But dear, I..." Mildred hesitated. "You've clearly been hurt, or assaulted by someone. Do you remember his name?"

A name? She didn't remember anybody's name... She remembered... she remembered that man from the university — not Derek. His friend, Eddie. He was standing over her. Telling her she needed to fight. That was the last image she had.

She didn't even know how long ago that was. She didn't even know how long she had blacked out for.

"What date is it?"

"Why, it's the eighth of December." Mildred glanced at her husband, who sat back in his chair with his arms folded.

"The eighth?" Kelly tried to remember the last date she remembered… when Eddie spoke to her. She recalled the day before being moved to a psychiatric unit, that was the fifth, meaning that day was the sixth. Had she been out for almost forty-eight hours? What the hell had happened to her? How did she not know what had happened in two day's space of time?

She placed the mug on the table. She was distraught enough and this couple were staring at her, which was only adding to her stress.

"Can I use your bathroom?" she requested.

Mildred nodded and pointed through the hallway.

Keeping the jumper wrapped around herself, she huddled her way into the bathroom, closed the door behind her and locked it.

She watched herself in the mirror. She was a state. Soil stuck to her forehead, dried sweat in her hair, scratches on her face and her neck. Whatever it was she had done, it had left her marked, sweaty and naked.

"But we have to phone the police!" she heard Mildred whispering all too loudly from the front room. "She's clearly been raped or something. What else are we supposed to do with her? And, what's more, you have a whole field of cattle out there slaughtered!"

"I know, dear." Bill's voice joined her, sounding far calmer and less frantic.

Kelly opened the door to the bathroom and hobbled back down the hallway. She saw Mildred with the phone by her ear, her hand halfway through dialling; she poised mid-air as soon as she saw Kelly re-emerge.

"Dear, I was just ringing the police."

"I said not to ring the police," Kelly said expressionlessly.

"I know, dear, but we just think it's best."

"Put the phone down."

Mildred froze. Was she threatening her? Kelly's voice was

so flat it was hard to tell whether she was aggressive or vulnerable.

"Are you sure?"

Without any warning, the phone flew out of Mildred's hand.

Mildred's eyes widened and her mouth dropped.

"How did you-"

The phone rose into the air and the wire between the landline and the receiver stretched out. Mildred watched it hover in front of her eyes, then, before she knew what had happened, the wire flung itself around her throat, wrapping numerous times and squeezing.

Bill jumped up and thrashed at the wire, urgently attempting to peel it off, putting all his strength into it, trying with desperation to stop his wife from suffocating.

It was no good.

The wire was wrapped too tightly around her throat and there was no way he could stop it.

"Stop it!" he demanded of Kelly. "You're killing her!"

Kelly looked blankly back.

Bill jumped up and charged at Kelly. Before any sound could come out of his mouth, Kelly had lifted her hand and he halted.

She tilted her head and looked deep into his eyes. Those old, aged, worried eyes.

She squeezed her fist tighter and tighter. He grabbed his chest in response, feeling it tighten, clutching as hard as he could.

It was no good. He was helpless to stop.

She opened her fist. He gave a final whimper before his heart exploded, then his body fell limply to the floor next to that of his dead wife.

Kelly trod over them as she made her way toward the door, taking the farmer's car keys from the bowl as she left.

CHAPTER TWENTY-FIVE

*E*ddie and Derek sat at the table in Derek's home study in tedious silence, their heads buried in their hands. Since they were no longer welcome at the university, they had to make do with a room in Derek's house. Despite being in more cramped conditions, the shelves held a generous library with enough books about demonology and the study of the paranormal to put Eddie in awe.

But Eddie had no time for complimenting Derek's book collection; not on this day, not at that moment. It had been two days since they had witnessed the first death they had ever seen during an exorcism. They had never known a demon that possessed its victim with such control, allowing them to wield the kind of power that allowed them to kill someone from across the room. It was worrying. No, worrying was too light – Eddie found it petrifying.

It was the first time they were up against something that could more than match him.

What's more, there was a feeling in Eddie's gut, plaguing his mind; the feeling that Eddie had something to do with this evil entity. It had looked at him, directly at him, and said, "Come find me, we have much to do." Why would Eddie try to find him? What was it they had to do?

Most of all, the question at the forefront of Eddie's mind was: *Who the hell am I?*

Derek seemed to be in denial, refusing to be drawn into a conversation about it, denying any possibility as soon as the subject came up. Eddie had never seen him like this. Derek was normally so wise and approachable, he had taught Eddie so much.

"I'm going to get a drink," Eddie said.

Derek grunted without lifting his head up, still in the dire state he had been in for the last forty-eight hours.

They had never seen a man's head get sliced off before. How were they meant to explain that? The police seemed more than sceptical when they told them a nineteen-year-old girl had done it, then escaped through a window nine feet up the wall.

Eddie trudged through the corridor, marvelling at the sculptures and art decorating the walls either side of him. It was a poor distraction for his mind and it didn't work, but Derek's décor was impressive nonetheless.

Then he saw a picture on a bookcase beside the kitchen entrance. A picture he had never seen before. It was small, discreet, out the way. He had rarely been to Derek's house, and when he had, it had been in a hurried rush whilst fighting a demon, leaving him little time to wander its halls.

The photo certainly raised more than a few questions.

In it was Derek, a younger Derek – with his arm around a woman. A beautiful woman; Eddie couldn't help but notice how striking she was. Her long, black hair glided off her shoulders and her smile was instantly engaging. She was resting her head against Derek's shoulder, who was smiling too, in a way Eddie had never seen him smile before — and he looked happy. So happy.

And on Derek's hand was a ring. Eddie had never seen an item of jewellery on him, but sure enough, there was a gold band around his wedding finger. He had never seen this woman, or even heard of her before.

And it was safe to say, as long as Eddie had known Derek, he had never seen a ring on his finger.

Shaking his head to himself, he left the photo and meandered into the kitchen. It's amazing how you can work so closely with someone, know so much about them, have so much dependence on them, yet not know one of the most important things about their life.

Where was this woman now?

He grabbed himself a tumbler and poured a small drop of whiskey in it. He had fully intended to have a coffee, but he didn't care at that precise moment about what time of day it was or what kind of standards he would be dropping; he needed it. The harsh hit of the kick against the back of his throat did the trick, if only fleetingly.

He opened the cupboard to find the coffee. There wasn't any. How did someone get through the day without coffee?

There's two strange things about Derek I didn't know.

Eddie filled up the tumbler once more and stepped out of the kitchen. He didn't want to join Derek in the study. He didn't want to sulk in the air of misery that hovered around Derek, so he dragged himself into the living room and turned on the television. At least Derek had a television. He felt like the kind of guy who wouldn't, for some reason, and Eddie was relieved.

Some cartoons were on ITV, so he flicked over to BBC2. Some tennis match was going on, with two women grunting as they hit the balls. Why did they always need to grunt? He flicked over once more to BBC1, where he found the news.

He decided he should probably watch the news. They were

going to need to go after Kelly, and there could be something on the news that gave them an idea where to look.

Oddly enough, he didn't have to wait long.

"And in other news, a couple were found murdered on their own farm, with their animals slaughtered, in a freak attack the police are labelling as unsettling."

"Oh shit," Eddie muttered, then shouted out of the room, "Derek, you're going to want to get in here, and fast!"

Derek joined him, watching with dismay in the doorway as the news reported the senseless killing of a whole farm of animals. Cows had been mercilessly slaughtered, as had sheep, and even the dog; some of which had been eaten, and some of which had their limbs stripped, torn apart, and strewn over the field.

The couple who owned the farm had been murdered; the man from a heart attack and the woman from asphyxiation. They were an elderly couple named Bill and Mildred Pearson, and the police were apparently considering potential avenues.

That meant they had nothing.

"Grab your coat," Derek spoke in a husky voice, as if he had a cold. "We need to go."

"Why?" Eddie rose and frowned at him.

"Because this was clearly our demon."

"Yes. And what do we hope to find there?"

"I don't know, a clue maybe? Somewhere she's gone?"

"And what then? What are we supposed to do then? You keep avoiding the conversation, Derek, but that thing killed a man without even touching him. That thing — spoke to me as if it knew me. Why?"

"I said I don't know-"

"And I say that's horse shit."

They stared at each other, tension rising. For the first time, Eddie was angry at Derek, and he wasn't even sure why or how to direct it. He just felt like there was something going on, something he wasn't telling him; he was too distant. Eddie was sure Derek knew something, but was unwilling to talk about it.

Derek just grabbed his coat and left. Eddie sighed. He knew he shouldn't be mad at him. Whatever Derek did, he did it with the best of intentions.

Eddie grabbed his coat and followed, closing the door behind them.

CHAPTER TWENTY-SIX

*B*erlinda typed the e-mail with difficulty, her new nails getting in the way. She would not remove them, oh no; she had spent too much money getting these nails put in, and as she admired the length of them stretching an inch away from her finger, she concluded they were worth the money. So, she kept stubbornly hitting the backspace key to remove her mistakes and type the error-filled sentence again.

Her fingers were too fat anyway, what difference did it make? Since her husband had left her, these nails were the only thing keeping her going and she would be damned if she was to remove them.

She gave her hair a nudge. It was moulded into a perfect afro on top of her head. She glanced at herself in the reflection in the computer monitor and smirked. She looked damn good and she felt it, possibly for the first time in a long time.

"Excuse me," came an impatient voice, prompting Berlinda to lift her head and recoil in horror at the audacity of someone addressing her so.

"Excuse me?" she replied, moving her head from side to side. "Excuse you."

184

"I need some help," came the voice of the timid boy in front of her. He was evidently a fresher, still young, and was yet to grow the confidence to stand up to the vain receptionist who would rather focus on her e-mail to the yoghurt company who had caused her fingers to become unduly fat.

"Hello." She lifted her left eyebrow and tilted her head toward him to display her annoyance, needlessly elongated the "o" of "hello."

"I need an extenuating circumstances form for my assignment."

"And what is so extenuating with your circumstances you think you demand an extra week?"

"Er, well…" he stuttered, staring at his feet and wobbling from side to side anxiously. "I had to go home, my little brother needed me."

"I don't know if that's enough," she answered, the pitch of her voice rising at the end of the sentence as if it was a question. "Maybe you should go speak to someone who gives a shit."

Without daring to look her in the eye, he turned and shuffled away awkwardly, keeping his head facing the floor. Berlinda tutted to herself and turned back to her e-mail.

You said that your yoghurt had ftbt carbories.

"Fuck it!" she exclaimed, hitting the backspace once more. She loved those nails, but they were getting rather annoying.

"I need some help," came a blank voice that made Berlinda jump. Out of nowhere stood a young lady in front of her with a vacant expression. She had bags under her bloodshot eyes, her skin was overly pale, and she looked at Berlinda in a way that made her shiver.

"I, like, am totally sure you do, but as you can see, I'm doing something, and you proper made me jump."

"I need the home address for your lecturer, Edward King,"

she said monosyllabically without reacting to Berlinda's rude outburst.

"Right, yeah, sure you do. But there's a word beginning with *p* peeps say around here, maybe you should try it."

"I need the home address for your lecturer, Edward King," she repeated, with the exact same monotone voice.

Berlinda pulled her head back and frowned.

"Did you not hear me, I said-"

"I need the home address for-"

"Yes, I heard you the first time. We aren't really used to giving out the home addresses of our staff to our students here. I'm sure you can go see your professor on your own time."

The girl didn't move, didn't blink, didn't change expression whatsoever. She gazed into Berlinda's eyes and Berlinda grew increasingly uncomfortable.

She went to object again, but her throat tightened up. She felt it swell and swell, like her oesophagus was closing in on itself. She tried to speak but she couldn't, a helpless gasp coming out of her mouth instead.

All through this, the girl just kept staring.

After a few seconds of clambering at her throat with her oversized nails, she gasped suddenly, breathing in and in, feeling the press on her throat lessen and finally let her have more air.

"I need the home address of Edward King."

Berlinda nodded. She didn't know why she agreed to it, but she said, "I'll give you the home address of Edward King," and began typing on the computer.

The young lady took a post-it note from beside Berlinda's computer and placed it in front of her.

"You will write it on here."

"I will write it on here."

Once she found the address on her computer, she wrote it

down on the post-it note and handed it over, the whole time desperately thinking, *why am I doing this?*

"I don't know what the hell you just done, young lady, but you better learn some manners," she said.

The girl tilted her head and narrowed her eyes. Berlinda felt her own hands lift and her nails point toward her throat. She cried and whimpered as the thick, sharp, fake spikes attached to her fingers edged closer and closer to her neck. Slowly but surely, they pressed slowly into her skin. She felt blood trickle down her collar bones.

The last thing she heard was the thud of her head against the keyboard.

CHAPTER TWENTY-SEVEN

*E*ddie and Derek pulled up outside the farmhouse to find a barrier of yellow tape. They stepped out the car together and walked slowly toward the crime scene. There were Scene of Crime Officers in white protective outfits walking in and out of the farmhouse with bags of evidence. Officers were stationed by the door and at the edge of the police tape, creating a border between the crime scene and the horde of reporters who had gathered with their microphones and cameras.

"How the hell are we going to get close enough to see anything?" Eddie muttered to Derek, buttoning up his coat, feeling the cold winter air against his face. "What did we hope to gain from this?"

At that moment, two bodies were transported in body bags to the vehicles at the side of the house. Eddie was transfixed by the sight; he could feel the death underneath them.

"Perhaps you could help out there," Derek answered. "Can you tell us anything about those bodies using your gift?"

"I wish we'd stop referring to it as a gift, Derek. I think we both know it's far from a gift."

"Okay." Derek forced a fake smile, refusing to be drawn into an argument. "Can you tell us anything? Anything that will give us a clue as to the whereabouts of our demon?"

Eddie watched the bodies get loaded into the van.

"The first one was the man, the second was the woman. The demon did it, it reeks of it. I can feel it in my bones."

He wasn't lying. Everything he had felt when next to the demon inside Kelly's body was filling him up and spilling over like a jar of acid. His nostrils filled with a uniquely dusty scent, and the demon's anger and hostility filled his mind. This was more than the presence he felt with other demons. It was as if he was becoming the demon itself.

"Come," Derek suggested. "Let's see what we can make of the animals."

They followed the police tape to the adjacent field, where a few more people in white outfits retrieved samples and took pictures. Despite the barrier between them, they could see everything clearly. The cows were on their side, sheep on their back, their bodies slit open and their insides strewn over the field. There were very few patches of green left, blood having soaked into the grass in most places, often surrounding some body part, like an intestine or a liver.

Eddie could see it happening before him. He could see Kelly walking through the field, in the dead of night. She was naked. Her eyes were glowing, her hands were raised, and as she crossed each animal they were slit open in turn.

He saw another flash as Kelly ate their hearts, threw out their entrails, and fornicated with one of the corpses.

"What is it?" Derek asked.

"It's…" He wasn't sure where to start. "I can see it. Everything. Kelly was here, she did this, she ate their body parts, she mutilated them, she even fucked them."

Derek bowed his head. When he lifted it again, Eddie was flinching his face away, the visions in his mind too much.

"I think we need to be prepared, Eddie," Derek said softly.

"Prepared for what?" Eddie spat out, angrier than he had intended.

"For what this may mean. For the world. For you."

Eddie turned his back to the field and put his hands on his hips. He faced the woodland area, not wanting to look at the image of Kelly killing helpless animals, but also not wanting to look at Derek.

"I know you aren't particularly content with me right now," Derek said. "But we need to expect the worst about what this might mean."

Eddie ignored him. "Hey, Derek, were you ever married?"

Derek didn't move. He forced his face to show nothing, no hurt, no reaction whatsoever.

"What does that have to do with anything?"

"I have worked beside you for years, and I have never questioned anything you have told me, nothing that you have... Then I see a picture of you with a woman, in your house, and you have a wedding band on. How can I work so closely with a guy and not know something as personal as that about him?"

"You did not need to know."

"That's it, Derek." Eddie turned and jabbed his finger, avoiding the images of Kelly continuing out of the corner of his eye. "What else is there that you think I don't need to know?"

Derek put his hands in his pockets and looked away.

"Now's not the time, Eddie."

Eddie sighed and turned away, throwing his arms in the air.

"Eddie, we need to be together with this, don't turn against me. If this... thing... is, as it claims to be, the devil himself, then we are up against the epitome of evil. The living embodiment of everything that is bad in the world in the body of a helpless young woman. Whatever you are, whatever it is you have, the world needs it, and it needs it now more than ever."

Eddie lifted his head, his foot tapping unbeknownst to

himself, as he kept his gaze directed at the wood. He looked to the house.

He saw Kelly leaving it. He saw Kelly pause, blood on her hands. The blood faded. She looked up.

He saw her mind. He saw her thoughts.

"Oh my God." He felt sick. He turned to Derek with an immediate sense of terror. "I know what she's after."

"What?"

Eddie closed his eyes and took a deep breath in.

"Me."

CHAPTER TWENTY-EIGHT

*T*he rough cement under Kelly's bare feet caused her no pain, despite the blood patches trailing behind her. Those patches were soon washed away with the rain, a belting barrage of water that didn't bother her in the least.

She paused beside a building, looking up at the fifth floor. This was where she needed to go.

The door was locked. She didn't care. She pressed a random buzzer on the intercom pad in front of her and was greeted with a poorly sounded "Hello."

"Open the door," she spoke, and they complied without hesitation. It buzzed open and she entered, walking straight to the lift.

As she pressed the up button, a man in a suit walked up to her in a fizz, taking down his umbrella and shaking his jacket out. They entered the lift together. She pressed floor five, he pressed floor six.

"It's mad out there," he observed, making chitchat. "I'm drenched."

Her head turned and glanced at him, at this street urchin that dared speak to her. Did he not know who he was underneath the young, attractive, female exterior? Sure, he may be looking at her as a young lady he could idly flirt with, but it wasn't so.

Not for the first time, it became disgusted with the body it had chosen. It needed a weak-willed, vulnerable young adult, and it had chosen a sack-of-shit girl who was too pretty for her own good.

"Hey, I haven't seen you before," he sweetly smiled at her. "You new to the building?"

Kelly threw her arm forward, upper cutting him with the palm of her hand, sending him clashing against the ceiling of the lift and collapsing on the floor in a lump.

The door pinged open and it stepped over the mess and entered the corridor. It made its way down the dimly lit passage, lights above flickering as it passed. It reached the intended room and without needing to move an inch, sent the door flying off its hinges into the distance.

It entered and switched the light on. The fluorescent light flashed on and off rapidly in reaction to its presence. With a flick of her hand, it forced all the lights around the room to burn out.

There was no one there. The presence it was after was not present. This search was taking far too long and impatience was beginning to grow.

Kelly felt herself being dragged for a moment. She was inside her body. She could feel the anger, the hostility, consuming her, but she was not in control. She was in there somewhere, but lonely, scared, in the corner of the mind.

It picked up a picture from the bedside table. It was one of many scattered around the flat that featured Eddie and two women. One blond, one brunette, both cuddling each other intimately, occasionally with their arms draped around Eddie.

It took in the photo. It consumed everything about it; not

just the image, but the feelings associated with it; feelings of love and caring. It was repulsive.

Lifting the photo to Kelly's nose, it sniffed, taking in the scent; light perfume and non-bio washed clothes, a hint of lavender air freshener. The history of the photo. It had been taken on a picnic, a few years ago. And the women. They were in love.

And with that, it could feel that love, it could feel those women, it could smell them, like rotting or potent chemicals. It took it all in, filling its body with it. It gave it direction. It gave it a path to follow that would lead to these women.

They were the key. They were the ones Eddie cared about most. If it found those women, it could draw Eddie to it.

And it knew where they were.

CHAPTER TWENTY-NINE

*J*enny practically floated downstairs, despite a quick stumble that wasn't so elegant. Her legs were still weak and she could still feel Lacy on her tongue.

She perched at the edge of the kitchen and closed the blinds, ensuring the neighbours didn't see her nudity. They had no doubt heard what she had been doing; didn't mean they needed to see it too.

The coldness of the kitchen floor startled her, so she tiptoed to the kitchen and opened the fridge.

"Hey, Lacy?" she called out.

"Yeah?"

"Where's the beer?"

"Bottom shelf."

She reached to the back of the bottom shelf, withdrew two bottles of lager, and closed the fridge door before getting a bottle opener.

She paused, listening to the rain pounding against the window. She hadn't noticed it was raining, having been otherwise occupied. She opened a gap in the blinds with her fingers and peered out at the late afternoon sky. It was getting dark early; winter had definitely arrived. She was glad she was inside, warm and cosy, with the one she loved.

She couldn't help but smile. After more than ten years and despite all the things they'd faced — including the prejudice they'd come up against and the unacceptance from their families — they were still going strong, still desiring each other as much as they ever had, and still feeling as strongly as they ever did.

She knew she was far more highly strung than Lacy, and that was fine. That was why they worked so well. Lacy kept her grounded, kept her calm, showed her a way of viewing the world that she would never ordinarily see.

A loud knock on the door made her jump and abruptly ended her thoughts. Who on earth could that be now? It was a long time since Eddie would be banging on their door in a mess, and there was no other person she could think of.

The knock sounded again.

"Hang on!" she shouted, looking around for something she could put on.

She found a dirty shirt in the basket beside the washing machine and shoved her arms into it as she scurried to the door. The knock banged out again as she quickly did up the buttons.

Lacy appeared at the top of the stairs. "Who is it?" she asked.

"Don't know."

BANG BANG BANG BANG.

"All right, all right!" Jenny blurted out, finally doing the bottom button up. Her legs were still on show and her breasts were quite clearly outlined, but she would still be able to keep herself covered by standing behind the door.

She took off the chain and opened the door, just slightly, leaning her head through it and keeping the rest of her concealed. Before her stood a young woman, hair drenched, bare-foot, gushing blood that was washed away in the rain. She looked empty, like her eyes had nothing behind them.

"Can I help you?" Jenny enquired.

"Edward King," the woman spoke in a blank tone of voice, then looked back at Jenny expectantly.

"Er, Edward King hasn't lived here for years, but I'd be happy to pass a message on for you."

"I need you to get him here, now," she said. Her voice didn't suit her; it was unnaturally low and aggressive, like it was being spoken by something entirely different. Knowing what line of work Eddie was in made Jenny become immediately unsettled.

"I think it's best that you leave," she concluded, as Lacy edged down the stairs and appeared beside her. She went to close the door, but without any movement from the woman, it flung wide open, forcing Jenny and Lacy onto the floor. Rain forced its way in from behind the woman, who stepped over the threshold and peered around.

Jenny and Lacy backed away, stumbled to their feet and raced across the hallway, but were sent falling onto their knees by a huge surge of wind coming through the hallway and into their backs.

The woman glided forward and stood over them.

Lacy suffocated.

She didn't know how or why, but her throat was closing in and she was grabbing at it, frantically, desperately. Jenny's eyes shot up at the woman, taking Lacy in her arms and stroking her hair.

"Let her go!" she demanded.

The woman sliced her arm downwards and Jenny felt a deep claw drag down on her face. It left a gash and she howled in pain.

Lacy could suddenly breathe again, and took in as many intakes of breath as she could.

"What do you want?" Jenny shouted above the deafening volume of the wind and the rain.

"Edward King," she answered. Then her head lifted and her eyes focused dead on something in front of her, something only she could see. "I see you."

CHAPTER THIRTY

The crime scene tape had only recently come down from around Mindy Parker's room in halls of residence. Eddie could still see the faint remnants of red over the walls and the carpet. Everyone in the flat block had since been moved to another to allow for investigation by the police, then cleanup by the university; cleanup that had clearly not taken place yet.

The window was shattered, and small shards of glass were still engrained in the carpet. The room had been stripped of possessions, but the unique smell of pain only present to Eddie stunk. He knew Kelly had been here, and he knew everything it had done in her body. The way it had taken control of her fury and viciously attacked her boyfriend and her best friend.

Eddie had read that Kelly's boyfriend, Doug, didn't even remember entering Mindy's bedroom. He claimed he had no recollection of how or why they ended up having sex, just that he was somehow there. Eddie had no doubt this was part of the plan all along; to latch onto the poor girl's anger and use it to take control. He'd seen it before.

Once he had finished in that room, he joined Derek in what

used to be Kelly's room. The bed was upturned and the wall was covered in morbid red writing. Writing that would have been covered up by the bed sheets, writing that had been previously concealed by the wardrobe and bags that Kelly had piled against the wall.

The writing was repetitive and gave Eddie no comfort. *My son cometh* was written over and over again in no discernible pattern.

Next to the words was some Latin. Eddie did not know Latin fluently, but he knew Derek did from his studying of the dying languages that demons used.

"What does it say?"

Derek bowed his head and rested his eyes. He was despondent, almost resolved with having to confide in Eddie the reality of the situation.

"Derek, knock it off, what does it say?"

"Ille cum inferno. It means…" He hesitated and looked up to the heavens. "He brings hell with him."

My son cometh. He brings hell with him.

Eddie stepped out of the room. He didn't make the conscious decision, it just happened. He couldn't stay in there, not with such a clear prophecy written on the wall that was blatantly connected with him.

Maybe he was just going to have to stop living in denial, as was Derek. Maybe he wasn't put on this earth for good.

But if that was so, why did he hate it this much? Why was he battling against such a destiny if he was meant for such evil?

If he really was the son of Hell, bringing Hell with him, the heir to all that is bad in the world, then why did he have a conscience? Why did he love? Why did he choose to battle the forces of darkness rather than join them?

He felt Derek's hand on his shoulder. He shook it off, taking a step out of his reach, keeping his back to him.

"I know you are pissed off with me about the whole thing,"

Derek admitted. "But I've been in denial about all this too. I want you by my side, fighting the evil with me. Maybe I was being selfish. If so, I apologise."

Eddie had never heard an apology from Derek. With a nod of his head, he turned toward him and, without a word being spoken, they shared a moment of silent reassurance; an understanding that they were on the same team.

"I-" Eddie went to speak, then froze. His body turned to ice. In a flash, he felt an extreme freeze followed by an extreme heat surge up his body.

He fell to his knees, crying out in agony. His head filled with swirling thoughts and images he couldn't make out, pounding against his skull harder than his heart against his chest. He could feel the cells in his brain throb. He could feel everything. He could feel...

Jenny. Lacy. They were in pain. He could feel it.

Then he saw it.

Kelly was at Jenny and Lacy's house. An image as clear as the hallway in front of him. The patterned wallpaper, the quaint crockery, the blood on the wall.

Blood?

Jenny was suffering. She was on her knees, bent over Lacy, whose neck was shrinking in on her, Kelly's hand reached out toward her.

"Let her go!" he saw Jenny shout.

"Stop!" Eddie screamed, and Lacy's throat was released.

"What do you want?" Jenny cried out, grasping Lacy's hand in hers.

"Edward King," Kelly spoke, but in a voice far deeper and unsuited to the body presented. Her face was pale, her eyes bloodshot and her pupils dilated. Her eyes settled on Eddie; even though it was in his mind, her eyes met his, dead set, looking directly into him. "I see you."

"Let my friends go," Eddie demanded, trying to force confidence into his breaking voice.

"Come join me. Or they will suffer."

And with that, the vision ended. Eddie collapsed into a ball on the floor, all the energy leaving his muscles, a lump of bawling mess crying out for his friends.

"Eddie?" he heard Derek's calm and measured voice. "Eddie, can you hear me?"

As Eddie's strength mildly returned, he sat up and focused on the room. The plain walls and old carpet came back into focus and he looked to Derek next to him.

"It's at Jenny and Lacy's house. It's going to kill them."

Eddie rose to his feet and stumbled forward. He used the walls to hold himself up and fell against the door.

"Eddie, stop." Derek rushed to his side, putting his arm out to balance him. "You are in no fit state to face it."

"I don't care. It's got my friends and I'm going after it."

Eddie attempted to push Derek off but just stumbled again, his knees giving way to his shaking thighs. He made it to the door and burst it open, holding onto it for support.

"Have you considered this is what it wants? You weakened, more easily influenced, bait in their trap?"

"I've still got to-"

"Got to what, Eddie, you're a mess! You can barely stand. This thing has killed people, for God sake! This isn't like anything we've come up against before. And it's your soul it may well need to claim this time, and you're just going to stumble in there and give it to them?"

"Go to Hell, Derek!" Eddie turned his head and screamed with all his rage. "Go to Hell! I don't give a shit about the world! Maybe it's not for me, maybe — but I will not rest while my friends die. You can help me or you can get out of my way."

Derek saw there was no stopping him, so he chose the latter. He scooped his arm around Eddie's shoulder and helped him on his way.

CHAPTER THIRTY-ONE

*J*enny and Lacy lay on the floor, blood dripping from their various wounds, their fractured bones confining them to each other's loose, cowering embrace.

Kelly's body barely resembled a young woman anymore, but more a morbidly ill, deformed monster. The bags under her eyes had grown darker, her pupils had dilated to the size of her eyes, and hair mixed with blood so thick it turned dark red. Her lips were cracked and peeled, her face pale and the skin of her body tight, thin, over rigid bones. Wherever Kelly was, she was buried deep within.

"May thy mercy, Lord, descend upon us!" Eddie's voice cried out as he burst through the door. He strode forward, his teeth clenched into a snarl and his frown full of fight.

"As great as our hope in thee," Derek answered, entering behind Eddie and staying out of the way.

"You came," it said.

"We drive you from us!" Eddie roared, disregarding the ache in his lungs and the scrape of his throat.

The demon stood no more than a yard away from him. His

outstretched arm pressed the cross toward the creature, who returned his stare.

The demon smiled at the sight of the cross burning in Eddie's hand, but Eddie ignored the warm tinge, overlooked the smoke protruding from his palm, and discounted the smell of his burning flesh.

"Whoever you may be, unclean spirit, all satanic powers, all infernal invaders, all wicked legions, assemblies and sects. Be gone, demon!"

The torrential storm outside bashed against the window. The lightning struck with the thunder. It was an almighty showdown between good and evil, the devil and the servants of God – the fight between Eddie and what lies inside; what had, up until now, remained dormant.

"Your hand burns by the cross," came the multiple voices combined into a tuneless chorus from Kelly's warped mouth. "And you still think you are one of them?"

"Demon, your name?"

"My name is Lucifer. Satan. The devil himself. And I am no demon."

"In the name and by the power of our Lord Jesus Christ-"

"I am your lord!" bawled the demon, trembling the house, the cracking of an earthquake beneath their feet. A tree branch collapsed through the window, recurring flashes, thunder and lightning persistently pounding against the house.

"You are not my lord, you ignorant bastard!"

"You exorcise me like you would a demon. I am no demon. I am a fallen angel. I am a ruler of demons, a king of the kings, I am the god of Hell!"

"Then, god of Hell, you will leave this servant of our Lord, Jesus Christ, and be banished back to where you came from!"

"You think your name is Edward King? That is not the name I gave you."

Eddie glanced over his shoulder at Derek. A different name? What was it on about?

"Don't listen to it, Eddie. Remember what you tell everyone in an exorcism. It will say whatever it must to deceive you, just continue."

Eddie twisted back to the demon. It appeared amused. Smirking at him, breathing intensely, uncomfortably still.

"He knows, you know. Your friend, Derek."

Eddie let the statement echo in his mind for a moment. Then he remembered what Derek had said. He must continue the exorcism, no matter what.

"The most high God commands you, leave this body."

"Derek knows. He's known all along. He read the prophecy. He read that this would happen."

He didn't look over at Derek. He didn't need to. He would not be tricked.

"God who wants all men to be saved and to come to the knowledge of the truth."

"Ask him. He read that you would be born as the devil's son and some-day would have to command Hell. He won't lie. Not now."

Eddie paused. He looked at Derek.

Derek looked back at him, a lost look on his face.

"Is that true? Derek?"

Derek bowed his head.

"You lied to me?"

Derek said nothing.

The laughter vibrated through Eddie's spine, his face scrunched up with tears and anger.

"You see, it's true," spoke the devil. "You are my son."

CHAPTER THIRTY-TWO

"You lied to me?" Eddie cried at Derek, his eyes breaking.

"Don't listen to the demon, Eddie. It's the basics."

"*Don't you dare tell me how to do my own job!*" Eddie screamed so hard he ended up coughing. "Did you lie to me?"

The demon smiled. Derek bowed his head. Eddie closed his eyes and pulled his face away from either of them.

"So you understand," the demon continued, determined, its deep, booming voice filling the room. "You know where your place is in this world."

"My place in this world," Eddie stood up straight, raising his posture, feet shoulder-width apart, "is between *it*, and *you*."

The thunder and lightning struck again, the thunder a constant rumble, and the lightning a constant blinding flash. Broken glass sailed around on the torrential wind, a tornado of objects surrounding them.

Kelly's unrecognisable form lifted into the air before Eddie.

Its mouth upturned. It grew angry. Its calm demeanour had ceased, and the room burst with chaos. Eddie clung to the wall to avoid getting swept away in the wind, continuously rubbing the rain-water out of his eyes.

He took a quick glance at Jenny and Lacy laid on the floor beneath the window, cowering behind Derek's feet.

Derek looked weakly back at him.

Eddie turned and faced the demon.

"You do not scare me," he lied.

"Fool. You think those powers came to you naturally? You think you were born with them?"

"I don't give a shit where you say they came from. I have used them to command all of the demons you have sent here out of the bodies of innocent people, and I will use them to do the same to you!"

"No." The elements grew angrier, with more vigour, more hostility. "*I* gave you those powers. You can command demons with them because they are *my* powers. They stand no chance at controlling me. I. Control. Them."

Eddie shook his head defiantly. Whatever his gut was telling him, whatever his thoughts were screaming, however true it was, he was not prepared to just give in and let this creature take him.

"You may be able to control my powers..." he said, slowly and clearly. "But you will not be able to control me."

"Eddie!" Derek screamed out. "Remember — if your powers come from Hell, *that is where they are at their strongest.*"

Derek brushed himself down and gathered himself.

The mouth of the girl stretched open to almost the entire length of her body, jaw breaking and cheeks ripping apart. A scream soared through Eddie and sent him flying onto his back and across the floor.

Derek stepped toward the demon.

"Derek, what are you doing?"

Derek waved his hand at Eddie, ignoring his protests. The

demon grew an amused smile, the way one might when a dog did an endearing trick.

Eddie attempted to stand and pull Derek back, but the demon rose its hand and sent Eddie flying back onto his arse.

"Hah!" the demon said. "You think you stand a chance against me?"

"You don't control my powers!" Derek said. "You don't!"

The demon laughed even harder, in more pitches of voice than Kelly's vocal cords should be able to produce.

"And what powers are they?"

"I don't know. My experience at fighting your demons, maybe. My faith in Eddie that he is here as a force for good. My knowledge that we will not stop fighting until you are buried deep in Hell where you belong!"

"Derek," Eddie moaned, unable to hide his concern. "Stand down. You don't stand a chance."

"You should listen to your friend, little man."

"And you should listen to the power of God." Derek raised the cross and pointed it at the demon. "On my Lord, on my brothers, on my soul, I demand you, demon, be gone!"

"On your soul?" The demon tilted Kelly's weary head inquisitively to the side.

Eddie reached out for Derek, fearing the worst.

"Edward King." The demon focused its demented eyes onto Eddie's. "If you want his soul... come get it."

Kelly's body dropped to the floor. A huge cloud of black smoke rose out of her mouth and flew into Derek's open jaw. Derek's body straightened up and his faced filled with alarm, then Derek's body fell to the floor also.

A black cloud appeared out of Derek's body, entwined around a helpless white cloud, and lingered in the air for a moment. Eddie could swear he saw a mouth laughing within it.

Then the cloud flew downwards, beneath the limp bodies of Kelly and Derek, and the chaos stopped.

The rain stopped, the thunder went, the lightning ended. The room was quiet, calm, lucid. Jenny and Lacy rose their heads, clinging to each other, looking around themselves hopefully.

"Is it done…?" Jenny asked weakly.

"No," answered Eddie, transfixed by Derek's body. "Far from it."

He dropped to Derek's body and took him in his arms, shaking him. Derek remained limp. Derek's eyes were wide open but there was nothing inside of them. His heart was beating, his lungs were moving, but he was not there. He was vacant, empty, like a vase without a flower.

"Is he dead?"

Eddie shook his head, keeping his eyes latched onto Derek, aware of Kelly's limp body also laying next to him. He knew what had happened. He didn't want to, but he knew.

"So he's okay?"

"No, Jenny. He's not okay."

"But he's alive?"

Eddie stood with his back to them, refusing to let them see his face as tears gathered. He wiped his eyes and turned to his oldest friend.

"Derek's here. But his soul is not. It took it."

"Where did it take it?"

Eddie looked beneath him, unable to find the words.

Jenny stood and edged toward him, placing a warm hand against his back. Even though he had brought this all to them, risked the life of both her and the love of her life, let the entity wreck her home, here she was, still ready to comfort him in his time of need.

"I'm sorry for your house."

"Eddie, stop changing the subject. Where has this thing taken Derek?"

Eddie shook his head. He still couldn't answer. But as Lacy

stood, brushing the broken glass off herself, stroking her bruised neck and nursing her black eye, she answered for him.

"He's in Hell," she spoke. "Isn't he? I mean, his soul is?"

Tears filled Eddie's eyes once more and he kicked a broken piece of chair across the room. He stormed away from them, into the kitchen, wishing to be alone.

The soul of his mentor, his friend, was being tortured for an eternity in Hell, and he had just sat and watched it happen.

He didn't deserve his friends' pity.

CHAPTER THIRTY-THREE

*E*ddie hadn't moved for hours. He sat at the kitchen table, his hands in his hair, and an untouched tumbler of whiskey in front of him.

Jenny had finished patching up Lacy and was now watching him from the living room. Lacy lay on the sofa asleep, finally — she had been in so much pain and Jenny had prayed for her to finally get some rest. Now, as she glanced at the clock and saw it go past 1:00 a.m., she turned her concern toward her best friend.

She had never seen him stay this still for so long. Even the alcohol laid out in front of him lay unmoved.

And she was to say what to him? "Cheer up, it's okay. Never mind." It would be ridiculous to think there was even a word that would change how he must be feeling.

The Eddie of a few years ago would likely have destroyed the kitchen in a drunken rage. Not now. No, he kept it all inside, and honestly, she wasn't sure that was any better.

Eddie knew she was watching him. He could feel her eyes burning through the back of his neck, he just didn't know what to say. If he moved, he would shake. If he spoke, he would cry. If he thought, he would have to face what he had let happen.

He felt Jenny's hand on his back, her reassuring touch providing a small comfort. Then he remembered what had happened. And the touch didn't work anymore.

She sat opposite him, slowly and surely, keeping her eyes focussed on his. She reached her hands out and rubbed his arms.

"It's not your fault," she told him.

Mistake.

He finally moved, but only to flinch out of her grasp and "tfft!" out into the air around him. He shook his head and leant back in his chair.

"You did everything you could, Eddie," she persisted.

"Yeah…" Eddie went to reply, but what was the point? His mentor was gone, and the last thing Derek saw was Eddie's disappointed face.

"It's not your fault he died."

"Died?" Eddie said. "Derek hasn't died."

"But, his body…"

"The demon in that girl, it was the devil. He didn't kill Derek, he took his soul."

"Where did it take him?"

Eddie went to answer, but didn't. A sudden thought came to him.

He stood.

He had an idea.

"I need to get there."

"Where? To Hell?"

Eddie nodded.

"Are you crazy?"

"I've been there before, Jenny."

"So? It's not like going on holiday to Florida, for God's sake.

We are talking about going to the underworld. Surely if the devil had that power here, then down there…"

Eddie froze. That was it. Of course!

"What?" asked Jenny, seeing a change in Eddie that she couldn't understand.

"That's it…"

"What?"

"I'm the son of the devil. I'm the heir of Hell."

"Er… what?"

"I'm supposed to take his place as the king of Hell. I'm supposed to rise up in the new millennium and take it, that's why I'm here."

"Okay…"

Eddie walked back and forth, his hands gesticulating in the air, buzzing, almost giddy.

"I can't beat him here because his power outdoes mine. It keeps happening; that's why I couldn't exorcise Kelly."

"So you think you'd have more power than the king of Hell in… Hell?" Jenny pulled a bizarre expression, shaking her head — what was he on about?

"Yes! If I am the heir of Hell, then I am supposed to take his throne. So I must be able to defeat him in Hell to do that."

"But, Eddie…"

Jenny was wary; she didn't want to take him off his high and bring him back down to earth, but she needed to.

"What?"

"What if you do defeat the devil, then won't you have to become the ruler of Hell?"

Eddie's stomach churned. She was right. He was torn. What if he ended up becoming the evil thing he meant to become in doing this? What if the devil knew that all along?

What if that's why it was luring him down to Hell in the first place?

No. Derek needed him. He had no choice.

"I'm going to Hell," he told Jenny, and raced into the living room, thinking desperately about how he was going to do it.

Jenny followed him. "How?"

He turned to her. A thought struck him. That was it.

"I need you to suffocate me," he said, and Jenny looked horrified. "I need you to strangle me until I'm on the verge of death."

"No no no no no no." Jenny shook her head, walking away from him, shaking her hands in the air, adamantly defiant.

Eddie rushed up to her and grabbed her arms in his hands, rattling her until she looked at him. She finally did, but with her head vigorously shaking and a constant whisper of the word no. She looked like a wounded child, so innocent. Eddie had forgotten; she hadn't been a part of this. She had heard the stories, but she had never been part of them. She had never witnessed the demons that tormented their victims that he had to fight.

It caused a pain in his chest to see her like this. To see her looking like a helpless child, wounded, delicately defiant.

"I know it's hard, Jenny. I know it's a lot for me to ask."

"Eddie, you are asking me to kill you!"

Eddie shook his head. There was no other way he could do it.

"You need to be strong."

"You are asking me too much."

"I'm not asking you." Eddie looked deep into her eyes, pleading with her. "The world is asking you. For so long the devil has stayed hidden. What if he won? What if he ruled?"

She shoved his hands off her and charged to the other side of the room, keeping her back to him, wiping away tears. She saw Lacy out of the corner of her eye. Laid on the sofa so peacefully. Physically wounded, but unaware, somewhere in a dream, or in an empty slumber.

"Think of Lacy," Eddie said. "You saw what it did to her

when it was restricted by its human form. This thing has killed and tortured people. What if, next time, it came back and did that to Lacy?"

Jenny spun around, this time not hiding her tears. "That's not fair! What about what it does to *you*? What about if I lose *you*? What if you become the very thing you have fought against?"

He had no argument against her. Whilst he knew it was the right decision, he knew the risks, as well as she did.

"I don't have any choice," he said.

Jenny folded her arms and stood defiantly. Eddie could still sense a weakness in her convictions. She knew, as well as she could, he had to do it.

She just didn't know if she could.

Eddie tore the telephone wire out of the wall, then ripped it out of the phone, stretching it out in front of him. He checked its length. It was long enough to go around his neck twice. He took a feeble step forward and reached it out to Jenny, beseeching her with those eyes.

So much about him had changed in the years, but those eyes had stayed the same.

"Jenny... please..."

Jenny huffed. She reluctantly stepped forward, holding out a limp hand, and took the wire loosely in her palm.

Eddie sat down and turned his back to her. He straightened his back and his neck, and waited. He knew it wouldn't be instant. He knew she would have to gather her strength. So he was patient. He closed his eyes, kept his neck straight, and waited.

Jenny stretched the wire out in front of her and went to place it around Eddie's neck, then withdrew it. She recoiled, powerless, fiddling with the wire.

"I don't know how to do it."

215

"It's easy. You just tie it around my neck as many times as you can, take the ends, and tighten."

"Tie it around and tighten…"

"Then you close your eyes, Jenny. You close them, drown out any sound and just concentrate on tightening them as much as you can. Put every muscle into it."

She nodded, slowly but definitely. She knew he couldn't see her, she just needed to acknowledge what he had said for herself.

She placed the wire delicately around his neck, wrapping it, then drawing it around once more. It hung loosely around his collar and she took the two ends in either hands.

"You're doing brilliantly, Jenny, you're doing so well. Now you just need to tighten it. Pull the two ends as hard as you can and don't stop until I stop moving."

He didn't want to do this. He truly didn't. Not just because of where he was going, but because it really, really hurt to die. Suffocating was a long, drawn-out process, and one that would give him a huge amount of pain.

But he needed to stay strong. Stay strong for Jenny. Or she couldn't do it.

Tears ran down her face. She was crying so loud that it was all that Eddie's could think about. She gave one quick tug and the wire tightened. It pressed around Eddie's throat.

"Harder…"

She tightened harder still, the tears falling, her head constantly shaking, flinching away, unable to look. If she didn't look at it, maybe she wasn't doing it.

She pulled and pulled as hard as she could. She concentrated on the pulling, clutching the ends in her hands, making sure they didn't get loose in her sweaty palms.

Her best friend. He'd held her hand when she came out to her parents. He'd hugged her when she cried about their dissatisfaction. He'd jumped for joy when she met Lacy.

And all she could now hear were the desperate gargles of him dying. The breath leaving, airless chokes spewing out of him like empty vomit, every last piece of oxygen escaping from his body.

It lasted longer than she thought it would. His arms hit out a few times. Not toward her, just in general. She pulled tighter, ignored what she was doing, pretending she was somewhere else. Somewhere she couldn't hear him attempt to take in air that wasn't there, again and again and again.

Then the sound stopped. His body went limp. Silence filled the room.

She opened her palms, releasing the wire from her hands. She didn't look at him. She didn't want to and she didn't need to. She just turned back into the kitchen and poured herself another whiskey.

She knew he was gone.

TIME AND DATE NON-EXISTENT

CHAPTER THIRTY-FOUR

"*Argh! Please, stop, let me go!*"

The scream was all Eddie could hear. His eyes hadn't adjusted yet. All he could see was orange blur. He could smell the burning ambers of fire, and the sound of angry flames beneath the sound of begging.

"*For fuck sake you have to stop!*" they continued. Lots of them. Multiple voices, coming from all directions; above, below, around.

Eddie knew where he was. He didn't need his vision to return to confirm it. He could taste the ash in his mouth, he could feel the heat against his skin. He had been here before. Only then, he knew nothing.

Now he knew everything.

Or so he thought.

"*Please, please, just stop hurting me…*" The cry was followed by the *tsst* of burning iron against skin and the stink of rotting flesh.

Eddie's eyes finally readjusted. His bones ached. His muscles were so weak. He lay flat on his back, his arms spread out, his face turned to the side, in agony.

Is this what Hell had done to him? Is this how the devil wanted him, weak and lethargic?

"*Let me go, please!*"

It was a woman's voice. She lay on the ground, metres away. She was unclothed, barely moving, crying. Bruised. Scarred. Above her, a horned beast lifted his fist up, held out his palm, and fire rose from it. With a sadistic grin, he planted his fiery hand upon her back.

"*Ah, no, please, stop!*"

Eddie rose to his feet and stumbled forward. He willed himself to appear strong, to at least seem threatening.

"Let her go," he demanded of the beast. The beast looked at Eddie and its eyes widened in shock. That shock turned to terror, then that terror transformed to pleasure. The demon was thrilled. In disbelief, unable to comprehend what he was seeing.

"You have returned…" It spoke in a deep voice, just like Eddie was used to hearing from possessed victims.

"Leave her be," Eddie replied, lifting his arm out. Without any intention of doing so, his arm sent shockwaves propelling into the chest of the beast, sending it flying off the edge of the stone cliff and into the lava below.

He looked at his hands. *How the hell did I do that?*

He hobbled over to the young woman, laying naked, humiliated and scarred, on the ground. He reached his hand out to help her up.

"It's okay."

Without any warning, the woman used her knees to propel her body forward and clamp her jaw around him. He screamed, and she did her best to cling onto him and take as much of a chunk out of him as she could.

He reached his hand out and she levitated in the air.

She was floating in the air.

He had done that.

How had he done that?

What the hell is going on?

She looked to him with hungry, sombre eyes, full of loss and fear. He knew she must be famished. He knew she had likely been tortured and starved and was desperate, but he couldn't help feeling furious at what she had just tried to do.

"Who do you think you are?" he spat at her. She panted, remaining silent. He knew he shouldn't hold it against her, but his blood still dripped from her mouth. In a burst of rage, he plunged his fist forward, forcing a hole through her belly, her guts spilling out, then waved his hands to throw her over the side and into the fire for an eternity of burning.

He stopped.

Oh, my God.

What had he just done? An innocent woman he could have helped, and he gutted her then threw her to the fire. His eyes closed and he shook his head.

Being in Hell is changing me.

He couldn't help it. He felt anger coursing through his veins, blood trafficking the fury around his body. He wanted to maim, to torture something. To take every piece of wrong that had been done to him in his life and make someone suffer for it.

He was the heir of Hell. He knew why he felt this way. He was in the place he was to inherit, if the prophecy was true. He couldn't let it win. He had to retain his humility, his dignity, his morals; otherwise, he would easily become one of them.

He would become the very thing he had spent his life defeating.

Derek. The mission. He needed to save his mentor, his friend. That's what he needed to focus on. Making sure he was not lost forever.

Still, he shook with rage. He felt as hot as the air around

him, as passionate as the fire licking at the side of the cliff, as dangerous as the burning of flesh that created the stink of Hell.

He could hear the screams. He could hear them all around him, crying out, begging for release, whimpering hopelessly for relief that never came.

He took it in with a big, inward breath. He enjoyed it. He thrived on it.

He wanted it to be his hands that tortured them.

He stepped forward, feeling the surroundings respond to him. Out of nowhere, the stone rose off the ground and manifested into an archway around him. He looked around himself, his eyes settling on the distant glow of amber filling the horizon, encompassing the horizon.

He had never felt at home before. Never in his life had he felt he had belonged. Yet there, in Hell, stepping forward, he finally knew what it was to know where he was meant to be.

I could get used to this, he thought with a menacing grin.

A demon scattered out in front of him, muscular and horned. As it noticed Eddie, it bowed faithfully on its knees.

"Master, we are glad you are here," it spoke to Eddie's feet. "I have been told to bring you to him."

"Good," Eddie said. "Take me to him. Take me to my father."

"Beware of the false prophets, who come to you in sheep's clothing, but inwardly are ravenous wolves."
    (Matthew 7:15)

CHAPTER THIRTY-FIVE

*J*enny didn't move from the floor. She couldn't. If she moved she would see his body propped up limply against the seat.

She kept her forehead pressed against the carpet, her hands behind her head with her fingers interlocked, balanced on her knees. It became uncomfortable, but she stayed there, stationary. The only things that moved were her shoulders, shuddering up and down in time with the sound of her crying.

"Jenny...?" she heard from behind her. It was Lacy's feeble voice. She had no idea what had just occurred.

"Lacy..." Jenny muttered between tears. She wanted to look at her. She wanted to sit up and rush to her arms, but she couldn't.

She might end up looking at him.

"Oh my God, Jenny!" Lacy cried out and Jenny heard her footsteps scarper past her. "Eddie's not moving!"

"No, stop!"

Jenny leapt up, keeping her back toward Eddie's body. She put her arms around Lacy and dragged her into the kitchen, slamming the door behind her.

"Jenny, what…?" Jenny put her arms around Lacy. "Jenny, you're hurting me."

Jenny had forgotten, Lacy had been hurt. She slid out of her embrace and looked at her. Dried blood stained her face. She was pale, and she appeared to be limping.

"Sit down," Jenny spoke softly, still wiping tears out of her eyes. She ran her arm along Lacy's back, attempting to show her with affection how glad she was to have her there. She loved her so much, and she was terrified. But she couldn't tell her that. Not at that moment.

She turned her head away and opened the kitchen cupboard, taking out antiseptic cream, a few wet wipes, and some plasters. She placed them on the table and looked at Lacy, who seemed confused.

"You've been hurt," she informed her. "The blood has dried. I need to deal with it."

Lacy nodded vacantly. She kept her eyes on Jenny, not sure what to make of her. Something had happened. She had seen Eddie's body sitting limply, vacant. Jenny was clearly distraught, and tears were still falling from her eyes.

But she didn't ask. She knew it wasn't the right time. She needed Jenny to deal with her emotions first. So she just sat there, letting Jenny wipe her face with one hand and lovingly brush her hair back with the other.

Lacy flinched slightly at the sting of the wet wipe. The blood had crusted over her wound and it took a bit of wiping for Jenny to clear it off.

"Jenny?" she said, still staring at her, still waiting for the right time.

"I know, Lacy. Please, just…"

"Just what?"

Jenny shrugged her shoulders. She sat next to Lacy and took her hand in hers, placing the nursing kit down and adopting a more intense look.

"We need to perform some kind of exorcism, or ritual," Jenny began, with energy she had not had a moment ago.

"For what?"

"For Eddie."

"Jenny, I think he's dead."

"Yes, he is, but…" How was she supposed to explain this to her? "But he's not just dead. He's in Hell. We need to bring him back. We need to restore him to his body."

"Why?"

"Because I don't think he'll find a way back otherwise."

"But, Jenny, we don't know the first thing about that kind of stuff."

Jenny sat back and turned her mind to deep thought. Lacy was right. She didn't stand a chance at even attempting to do what Eddie did. But maybe she didn't need to. Maybe this didn't require spiritual means. Maybe they could do it themselves.

"Fine." Jenny turned to Lacy. "We're going to resuscitate him our way."

"Jenny," Lacy stuttered, turning instantly weak. "I can't…"

* * *

THREE DAYS Earlier

LACY BURST into the toilet and locked the door behind her. Her scrubs were splattered with blood. She couldn't take this anymore.

She rushed to the mirror and turned on the tap, splashing a handful of water into her face. She kept it running as she splashed another and another handful of water over her. Anything to snap her out of it.

She lifted her head and considered her reflection in the

mirror. This was too much. She had taken on too much. Jenny was wrong, she couldn't do this. Her parents were wrong.

Everyone was wrong.

But what was she supposed to say? "Sorry, Dad, I understand you paid my tuition fees in order for me to do my master's degree in medicine. I apologise for having to pay out all of your savings in order to support me going through nursing school, but I can't take it anymore. I'm going to quit."

No, she couldn't. Especially when he had given up so much to help her. He'd said he'd known, when she was a child, as young as five, dressing up as a nurse and providing imaginary care to her mum, who was desperately ill. She didn't save her either, but then again, she wasn't a real nurse at the time.

Was she even a real nurse now?

Looking herself in the eyes, she struggled to focus her vision. It was out of focus. Her head was scattered, her thoughts all over the place.

Just two days ago she was talking to him, and he was fine, and he was just sat there, laughing and smiling with her. Joking. Absolutely fine.

But she couldn't resuscitate him. She was the first one in, it was up to her. By the time her mentor and the doctors had arrived he was dead, it was done.

They told her it wasn't her fault, that she did all she could do. She didn't buy it. A more experienced nurse, a better nurse, would have saved him. They would have done it.

She did exactly as they had trained her. Opened the airways, pinched the nose, breathed in... She'd tried cardiopulmonary resuscitation too, starting with the standard chest compressions.

But she hadn't remembered to check the airway. So it had made no difference.

If only she had checked the airway.

The thought prompted her to fill with tears and she knew,

once they started, she couldn't stop them. She sank against the wall and sloped down to the floor, burying her head in her hands.

She would hand in her resignation in the morning, with immediate effect.

* * *

"Lacy?" Jenny shook her. "You know what to do."

"No, I don't, Jenny, I can't. I can't…"

"Lacy, look at me." She cupped her girlfriend's face in her hand, forcing her to look her dead in the eyes. "Yes, you might fail. But I definitely would. You're the only shot we've got."

Lacy stared back at her.

"Lacy, please, he's my best friend…"

Lacy saw the eyes of the one she loved above all others. The one who supported her unconditionally, the one who would willingly die for her. The one who still made her legs go weak.

"We've got to check the airway first," Lacy said. Jenny smiled and took her hand, taking her to Eddie's body.

CHAPTER THIRTY-SIX

*E*ddie dropped to one knee and bowed his head, closing his eyes in respect. Then his head rose and he bestowed his eyes upon the grand king of Hell before him.

The devil's true form glowed, giving off radiant heat. He rose above everyone, his skin pure blood-red, his vicious tail waving behind him with a sharp spike upon its end. Its eyeballs were black and its pupils were red, reflecting the surrounding fire. Eddie could only marvel at its magnitude and the evil it exhumed.

Beside his foot lay a crying woman, covered in scars.

"You have come," its voice boomed, echoing throughout Hell, over the sounds of screaming.

"I have," Eddie replied. "And I'm here to fulfil my duty."

"Eddie!" came a voice to Eddie's right. He slowly turned his head and cackled like a maniac at the sight of Derek's soul, represented in human form, fixed by hands and feet to a wooden board that stretched his body from limb to limb.

Eddie turned his smirk to the devil.

"Eddie, what the hell are you doing?" Derek cried out between cries of pain.

"Why is he still here?" Eddie spoke blandly.

"A test, my son."

"A test? You need a test of my loyalty? Truly, with me standing here?"

"Forgive me, but you have been with the humans for so long, your human form has weakened you."

"I am free of my frail body!" screamed out Eddie in frustration. "I do not suffer the morals of fools!"

"Then destroy his soul, once and for all." He pointed his finger toward Derek, who was so full of wide-eyed terror. "For now, he could be resuscitated. Tear him into pieces so he suffers forever in Hell."

"Why him?"

"Because he kept you prisoner!" Flames sprayed into the air behind it as its blood-red skin became even bloodier, and its voice grew full of fury. "He kept you in the mortal world. He taught you to fight our demons. He told you that was the way. Prove your loyalty once and for all — *destroy him*."

Eddie's eyes met Derek's. The eyes of the man who had taken him when he was at his lowest and taught him how to use his gift, his burden. The man who showed him how to do all those great things he could do. The closest thing to a loyal father he had ever had.

"Very well," said Eddie, and he turned toward his former mentor.

"Eddie, please…" Derek sobbed.

"Close your filthy trap!" Eddie shouted and rose his hands in the air. The wooden board Derek was strapped to rattled. The devil closed his eyes, feeling the surge of power exuding from Eddie.

He threw his hands out, sending forward a surge of wind so fast it would be destructive to anything it hit.

CHAPTER THIRTY-SEVEN

*E*ddie's body lay on the ground, Lacy desperately pounding on his chest. Press, release, press, release, press, release.

She placed one hand on his forehead and two fingers under his chin, gently tilting his head back. Taking a deep intake of air, she put her mouth over his and released all the oxygen from her lungs. She drew her head back, took another intake of air, and blew into his mouth once more.

She shifted back to his chest, sweat dripping from her forehead and her fingers clamming together. She placed the palm of her left hand underneath her right and interlocked her fingers. She made sure her fingers were away from the ribs, hovered them over his heart, and continued to press down vertically on his breastbone, again and again.

She glanced up at Jenny, who was pacing back and forth. She had her hands over her face and Lacy could hear her muttering, "Please, please, please," under her breath.

Lacy checked the clock. She counted down the last five seconds until the thirty seconds were up and moved back to his mouth. She pinched his nose, took a deep intake of breath and blew into his mouth. She left her hand on his chest, feeling it expand, then deflate once more.

But it stayed deflated. She tried again, breathing in, making his chest expand, then feeling it deflate. She left her hand there, in hope that it would expand on its own.

It stayed flat.

She looked up at Jenny, who still had her face covered.

"Jenny?" she said, too quietly for Jenny to hear, too scared to properly attract her attention.

"Babe?" she said, louder.

Jenny turned and looked at her. She shook her head, but Jenny did not look ready to hear that Eddie wasn't going to make it yet, so she tried again. She interlocked her hands once more and continued to press on his chest. She repeated the song *Staying Alive* in her head over and over, keeping in time with it, checking the thirty-second period on the clock.

"Lacy? Is it working?"

"I don't think…" She couldn't finish the sentence. She saw the look on Jenny's face and she couldn't say it.

Jenny shook her head, covering her face. "Oh no, please. Please…"

Lacy sighed. She kept going. Though she knew it was no good, she kept going. It must have been at least fifteen minutes he had been dead, and it was very rare for anyone to come back from this.

Least of all at her hands.

Thirty seconds up. She took a deep intake of breath, placed one hand on his forehead, two fingers under his chin, and exhaled into his mouth.

Jenny held her breath as she saw the air from Lacy's mouth make Eddie's chest expand. Then she saw it deflate and stay still. Motionless.

Jenny knew she shouldn't have done this. She knew it was the wrong decision. How had he persuaded her into this?

"Jenny, I don't think it's going to work."

Lacy knelt back. Looked at Jenny, still not ready to accept it.

For her sake, Lacy kept going, trying the chest compressions again.

Jenny fell to her knees and put her hand over Eddie's. So many memories she had of him, about to end.

Then she felt it. A twitch in his hand.

"Lacy!" she cried out, then Lacy looked up and saw it too.

There was hope.

CHAPTER THIRTY-EIGHT

*E*ddie threw his arms out and sent the surge of wind soaring at the devil.

The devil simply waved his arms away and shook his head pitifully.

"You did not fool me."

Eddie looked to the restraints around Derek's wrists and made them fall to the ground. Derek dropped to his knees, blood dripping from various parts of his body.

"I didn't think I had," Eddie said. "I know part of your evil is in me. I can feel it. It drives my powers. Every demon I fight can see my true form. But we are what we become by choice."

"You are wrong."

"Look at my hands." He lifted his hands up to show the burns on his palms from the flames he had produced from them. "This is not real; the rules of the natural world do not exist here. Yet my hands still burn. What you think I am can throw flames, but where I come from, flames burn us."

"I do not understand."

"Whatever we were made to be... some demon wielding fire at will... we still keep the parts of what we have become." He smiled, looking down at the burns that felt painfully warm in his hands. "And you can't change that."

"Then you will stay here forever until you become Hell!" it roared, its voice thundering so loud Eddie felt its reverberations in his bones.

Eddie hadn't thought this far ahead. He didn't know what he would do. The devil would keep him here, for eternity if it wished, until he became what he was supposed to become.

And he would stand no chance against him.

Then he remembered. The spell he had done with Jenny. The one that rose fire.

Derek's earlier words echoed in his head.

"Remember – if your powers come from Hell, that is where they will be at their strongest."

If his powers were at their strongest here, then surely...

He locked eyes with the devil.

He rotated his hands around each other, not taking his eyes off his opponent for a moment.

"Igne egredientur," he spoke. "Igne egredientur."

A flame sparked within the circle. This had happened before, it wasn't enough yet.

"Igne egredientur. Igne egredientur."

His fingers felt scalding pain. Light flickered around his hands. Flames appeared, small, a round ball of them, within the circle he was creating.

Then the ball of fire disappeared.

Come on, Eddie. Focus. This is where you are strongest.

"Igne egredientur. Igne egredientur."

The ball appeared again, this time larger, turning in circles, growing in size until it filled the whole space between his encircling hands.

He focussed his eyes fiercely on the devil and grinned.

"Et ignis furorem!" he spat.

With a sudden, jolted movement, he flew his arms forward.

"Converte ad lucemvitae!"

The fire flew from his hands in a grand burst of flames, consuming Satan and those that surrounded him. Eddie did not see what happened beyond the blaze, but he knew they were safe for a moment.

"Derek, grab my hand!"

Boom boom.

He felt something, in his chest. His heart. It was beating.

Boom boom.

He felt his lungs fill with air.

Jenny! You wonderful, smart woman.

From beyond the flames, a lasso flung toward him. He ducked, turning on his heel toward Derek.

He needed Derek's soul. He didn't know how long he had, but he needed to take him back.

He felt the flames flicker off the lasso at his feet. The devil withdrew it again and threw it out further. He could see it approaching him in the corner of his eye, feel its heat behind him, smell its burning.

Once it was around him, he belonged to Satan.

He would belong to Hell.

He jumped out for Derek, holding his hands out, about to reach him, when he felt the lasso tie around his ankle.

It had him.

He was dragged back slowly, but he put up as much fight as he could, clinging onto the dips of the stone beneath him.

"Derek, you need to grab my hand!"

Derek clambered forward, his legs unmovable, the power of his limbs having been taken from him.

Eddie could see Lacy in his eyes. He could see her above him. He could feel her hands against his chest.

"Almost there!"

Derek reached out again, but Eddie was dragged away once

more. He dug his fingers into the ground, resisting with all he had.

He could see Jenny above him. She was crying furiously, whimpering *please* over and over.

"You need to do it now, Derek!"

With one final push, Derek leapt out and took hold of Eddie's hand.

"Now close your eyes!"

The roar of the devil shook the ground, splitting it in two. The fire rose and encompassed them and he scrunched his eyes closed and prayed, then—

Then nothing.

No sound, no feeling, no pain.

Nothing around him but silence. He felt at peace, content, resolute.

He was snapped out of it with a large intake of breath. His eyes flew open. He breathed quickly and repeatedly, in and out, in and out. He did not let up. He took in as much oxygen as he could, feeling his head pounding, his heart beating, knowing he had been deprived of oxygen for a while.

He looked around. Lacy was sat over him, staring at him, her eyes hopeful. Jenny held his hand so tightly she practically broke it, but he didn't mind. She did not stop crying. She just stared at him, her face in a scrunched-up mess.

Eddie turned his head and looked across the room. Derek was there. He was laid on the floor in just as weak a position as Eddie, but he was there. Looking back at him. Smiling weakly.

DECEMBER 31ST, 2001

TWO YEARS SINCE MILLENNIUM NIGHT

CHAPTER THIRTY-NINE

*E*ddie thought Lacy looked quite cute in her nurse's outfit, her hair tied back and scrubs on. She looked professional in a way he had never seen before.

"Right, we're all done," she said as she finished his checkup and recorded his pulse on her form. "You're doing great. You seem to be recovering far quicker than a normal person."

"Well, that's because I'm not a normal person, remember? I'm the son of the devil."

She laughed as if he was joking and opened the curtain, allowing him to step out into the hospital wing. He strolled down a few curtains and peered into one.

"Knock, knock," he said.

"Come in," replied Kelly.

He opened the curtain and walked in. She was bruised. Her ribs were in a cast and her eyes looked drugged-up. Still, she appeared far better than she had done a few weeks ago.

"How are you doing?" he asked.

"Fine," she said weakly. "You know, if you keep visiting me like this, people are going to talk."

Eddie chuckled to himself.

"Well, we'd best not disappoint them. How about when you get out of the hospital, we go get a beer, go on a proper date?"

"Well, you saved my life, I guess it's the least I owe you."

"Until then, I guess you'll have to do with these awkward visits." He kissed her delicately on the forehead and sat beside her, taking the chocolate box he had bought the previous day and helping himself.

* * *

"So how's Kelly doing?" Derek enquired.

"Whatever do you mean by that? What are you implying?"

"I'm, er... I'm implying, how is she doing?"

Eddie nodded and put his feet up on the table of the office. "She's doing great. Few more weeks and I reckon she'll be out."

He looked around his office, then peered out into the lecture theatre. He didn't know how they had been cleared. He didn't know how the university board had decided to drop their investigation, but he was glad they had.

And, in all honesty, he thought the more they didn't ask about these rumours of a young woman claiming they'd helped her from being possessed by the devil, the better.

"So, Derek, I've got to ask, seeing as it's two years on from my first coming, so to speak," he said, glancing to the date of New Year's Eve in the calendar. "What did that prophecy say?"

Derek hesitated and looked to the floor.

"Derek, come on. I need to know."

Derek nodded and lifted his head up. He forced a fake smile and looked Eddie in the eyes.

"It said that you are to the devil as Jesus Christ was to God. That you were to bring forth the devil to this world. It said your powers were from a place of pure evil."

"Wow." Eddie nodded, trying to take it all in. "That all?"

"But it's only a prophecy," Derek offered softly, if only to himself. "It's open to interpretation. It's like you said, that might be what you are on this earth, but... well... you are what you have become, not what you were born to be."

They shared a moment of silence until Eddie sighed, took his feet off the table, and turned his body to Derek.

"But what if I'm not?"

Derek didn't have an answer, so he just let the question linger in the air.

They both watched the clock tick. They watched it tick from 11:56 p.m. to midnight, sharing mutual silence in the darkness of the office.

"Well." Eddie took a bottle of wine from his bag. "Happy New Year I guess. At least we're not spending this one fighting any demons."

He poured wine into a paper cup and handed it to Derek, then poured one for himself.

"What are we toasting to?" asked Derek, lifting his cup in the air.

Eddie considered this. What could they toast to?

"To the devil," he announced. "Wherever he is on this joyous night. He lost the battle and I'm sure he'll be wounded."

Derek smiled, but did not laugh. They both drank.

"This won't be over, you know," Derek said. "He didn't lose the battle. He just didn't want to kill you once and for all, so he went easy on you. He wants you for himself, to do his dirty work on earth."

"Oh, I don't know, I mean – God killed Jesus, right?"

"I'm being serious."

"I know you are. I know this isn't over. I'm not a fool."

"Good, I'm glad you know that."

"Oh, I do. He's got a Hell full of demons to send after me, legions of loyal beasts ready to die in his name and claim as many victims as he can."

"So what are you going to do about it?"

Eddie didn't answer. Instead, he finished his wine, screwed up his paper cup and threw it in the bin. He stood up and walked to the door.

"Where are you going?" Derek asked.

"Out. I could do with a proper drink. You coming?"

Derek nodded. He finished his cup of wine, screwed it up, threw it in the bin, and took his coat from the hook off the door.

"Where we going?"

"I don't know," Eddie answered. "But I guess we'll find out when we get there."

EDWARD KING

BOOK THREE

AN EXORCIST
POSSESSED

RICK WOOD

WOULD YOU LIKE TWO BOOKS FOR FREE?

Join Rick's Reader's Group for your FREE and EXCLUSIVE prequel to The Edward King Series at www. rickwoodwriter.com/sign-up